GW00689705

Long Knife

Jack Shaw had won a great victory for the Union, but at a terrible price. Now he was going back to the Hacienda Shaw to die in peace. But even as the Blue and Grey were tearing the nation apart, Long Knife and his Apaches had decided to win themselves an empire in the West. Shaw had no choice but to grasp life anew and fight again, to take on the cruellest, craftiest fighters in the world with a scratch collection of has-beens and leftovers, to save not only his country but also the woman he loved.

In bringing to life this saga of the bloody 1860s, Mike Stall has created a truly dramatic and compulsively readable yarn.

Long Knife

MIKE STALL

A Black Horse Western

ROBERT HALE · LONDON

ISBN 0 7090 7234 1

Robert Hale Limited
Clerkenwell House
Clerkenwell Green
London EC1R 0HT

Typeset by
Derek Doyle & Associates, Liverpool.
Printed and bound in Great Britain by
Antony Rowe Limited, Wiltshire

Contents

For W. A. B.

Prologue

1864

What should have been a sharp, snappy little action had degenerated into a siege when the Confederates dug hasty trenches to the east of Graylings Landing. The western side faced the river, already in Union hands, but no landing was possible in the face of the battery of howitzers the Rebs had emplaced.

Colonel Jack Shaw sat his horse just inside Foldes Wood, half a mile off the northernmost entrenchment and watched the infantry assault go in. Thanks to heavy Union riverboat activity, the Rebs hadn't been able to redeploy their howitzers but their two light field pieces and the musketry of the Confederate infantry in the trenches were taking a terrible toll of the blue-coated attackers. His job was to exploit any breach but to exploit it first you needed to have it, and the blue line was being thrown back. Two or three hundred dead already and there'd be as many screaming on the surgeons' trestle tables in a few hours, when their shattered limbs were amputated. General May would be sending despatches for more troops and, as likely as not, dismounting the 118th Volunteer Cavalry for use – and abuse – as infantry. If the fool had let him attack two days ago before the trenches were complete, it would be all over by now.

'Look, Jack!' Major Harry Norris said.

Shaw looked where his second-in-command was pointing. A depleted platoon of Union troops had reached and held the first line of trenches. Shaw made a decision.

'I'm going in, Harry,' he said. 'I'll take six troops. You follow up with the rest if we make it. If not, keep out of it.'

'But—'

'That's an order, Harry.'

Norris smiled suddenly. 'Good luck . . . sir.'

They were already at a gallop when they came to the beaten ground just before the trenches – riding around and occasionally over their own dead. He had been dreading case shot from the two field pieces but they hadn't even been brought to bear, and the musketry had been to little effect. He hadn't seen a rider fall.

The Rebs in the trenches were standing up now, not so much to fight as out of sheer surprise – a bitter little fight had been reinforced by over 300 men on heavy horses, their sabres flashing in the afternoon sunlight. The Reb infantry obviously hadn't known a cavalry force was in the vicinity and they didn't believe their rifles and bayonets would stop it. The trenches might if they were wide enough. . . .

They weren't. Suddenly they were across and the trench line was broken.

'Thorson – roll 'em up,' he yelled to the lieutenant in charge of D troop and then, as he had already decided, led the bulk of his force into Graylings Landing itself. Thorson was being left to speed up the inevitable: with Union infantry on one side of the entrenchments and Union cavalry on the other the line must collapse. But the Rebs might just make a stand in the town itself. Take that by a *coup de main* and there was nothing for it but surrender and the end of the bloodletting.

As they came to the rather paltry suburbs, he glanced back. Thorson was doing his job well. The two field pieces had been taken already. Now all he had to do was to take the howitzers and the Reb general's HQ and it was all over.

He hadn't had to use his sabre once – the grey soldiers had melted away before them. Not cowards – anything but – just overwhelmed. He could almost hear his West Point professor saying again: 'Cavalry is weak in defence, demoralizing in attack.' Except he was a Reb himself now. . . .

The silence was strange, broken only by the clatter of the regiment itself, the only way he knew they were behind him, for now he didn't wish to look back. Then they were on the streets of the town proper, spreading out like a flood and he saw the howitzers – just three of them, a short battery – and they were still facing the river!

And then they were on them. Nobody fired a shot. A Reb sergeant lashed out with a rammer but was cut down and then the other gunners threw down their carbines and spikes and raised their hands.

Shaw felt extraordinarily calm. He knew his pulse should be racing, that he should be exulting, yet he had felt more emotion on an exercise.

'This way,' he yelled, gesturing to the right with his sabre – the way to the Reb HQ if May's intelligence was right.

Hooves clattered on the cobbled street then they came to the square. He saw the Confederate battle flag over the portico'd building that had to

10

be the city hall and pro tem HQ. A cluster of Rebs stood by the doorway and for the first time he heard shooting. But the bullets had no effect.

He spurred his horse in their direction. It was almost over. In a matter of minutes he would be accepting the general's surrender and in this tiny bit of the war the bloody horror would be over.

They were almost there. He thought the little clump of men in grey were going to break and run but one of them raised a carbine. He heard the cap strike fire, saw the smoke and then the bullet hit his chest like a mighty hammer. He swayed back in his saddle, his arms flailing, the sabre clattering on the cobbles of the city square.

'They've killed the colonel,' he heard someone shout from behind. And then other voices: 'No quarter! No quarter!'

So the bloodletting wasn't over, he thought, not by any means. Odd that there was no pain, just shock. And then he realized that he wasn't mounted any more, lying instead on the cobbles with horses legs all around him, and then the aura of calm that had surrounded him from the beginning of the action suddenly disappeared. He heard the sound of battle – screaming, shouting, the rattle of musketry and even saw the flash of descending sabres. And suddenly the pain was

11

there, in his chest, as if someone was trying to rip out his heart by main force. It was unbearable and he didn't bear it: with relief he slipped into silence and darkness. . . .

Part One

The Stagecoach

I

Manuel Gonzalez leant on the corral fence, took out the cheap nickel-plated pocket watch provided by the stage company, and checked the time. The watch ran slow, though no more than five minutes a day, but even making allowance for that they had plenty of time. It would be old Collier driving today and he was pretty reliable – and never early.

Not that there was much for him to do until the coach actually arrived. The horses were already fed and watered. The work would fall mostly on Isabella. And while young Manolito was old enough to help a little with the horses Pedrita was still little more than a baby.

But Isabella never complained. She only smiled. Even when the little garden she'd planted out back had dried up in the summer heat she

14

hadn't wept. He was a lucky man.

It was true enough. His father had been a *peon* of the de las Casas, lived in a hovel he couldn't even call his own and scarcely seen meat on his plate from year's end to year's end for all he was a *vaquero*, guarding the thousand-head herd of the de las Casas.

He, by contrast, was, to all intents and purposes his own master – just so long as the horses were changed on time – and it was a pleasure to work with such fine beasts as the company provided. His children's bellies had never known hunger, nor would they, and every month there was silver in his hand. And he was a free man, not a *peon*. He was content.

He reached into his pocket for the makings – he had time for a cigarette – but stopped. Was that the sound of distant horses? He checked his watch again. It shouldn't be, not unless the watch was very wrong indeed and he didn't believe it was.

He listened again. He could hear nothing. He looked back along the trail, could see nothing. And then on impulse he looked over the dusty scrub-land to the north. Nothing.

He shrugged, rolled the cigarette and lit it. Shortly he would go and remind Isabella the stage was almost due but it was unnecessary. Everything would be ready. Isabella was a good wife, better than he deserved. He smiled to himself. He was more than content; he was happy.

He heard a sound from behind him but didn't turn; it would only be the wind rolling a tumble-weed. . . .

II

The stagecoach pounded up at him with numbing regularity. The heat and the dust didn't bother him. He came from this region and he was used to it. Besides, as he was now, heat was almost an essential to him. For as long as it lasted. . . .

'There's a stop coming shortly,' the fat man said, wiping his brow with a large red kerchief. 'We can stretch our legs at least.'

'Uh-uh,' the thin man agreed. One was a surveyor – the latter – and the other. . . ? Shaw tried to recall what he did. He ought to be able to remember, they'd talked enough for all he hadn't listened. The girl opposite him had hardly said a word, hadn't joined in when the two civilians had tried to get his opinion on how the war was going – he was still wearing his colonel's uniform. His only suit had been lost and there hadn't seemed

17

much point in buying another. He would have felt happier with captain's bars rather than the eagles of his temporary war rank but there had been no point in making that change either. He wasn't in the army anymore – medically discharged. He was no more entitled to the bars than the eagles.

He glanced at the girl. He half fancied he'd seen her before but her frosty demeanour hardly encouraged asking that question. And her accent was faintly Southern – the uniform could hardly have been endearing to her. Not that it mattered overmuch. Out West there was a kind of truce: the land would go to the victors in the Shenandoah Valley and in the meantime there were Indians, droughts and plagues of locusts to worry about, among other things.

A sudden jolt stabbed pain into his back. It must have shown on his face for the girl's eyes widened a moment.

'Don't ask!' he willed her and she didn't. He didn't want to lie, but neither could he tell the truth – I'm going home to die. It sounded pathetic; even worse, ridiculous.

He'd known it when General Dicken had visited him in the makeshift hospital in Graylings Landing – guardless and still wearing his sword. He'd obviously been given his parole. Besides, he and May were classmates at the Point. He'd seen it in eyes even before he spoke. Hell of a war when the cadets you teach end up following your precepts too well and you end up being beaten . . . all that, and pity, too.

I won, he lost, Shaw thought, but he gets to live another twenty or thirty years while I'll be doing well to make two or three months. A little longer, the doctors insisted, if only he'd play the invalid. But he wouldn't do that.

He gripped the stick propped against the seat and the side of the coach. There was nothing wrong with his legs but they'd given him it anyway and it was a help getting up, being up and staying up. With it, he needed no man's hand to help him.

Caroline Lawton had to work hard not to stare at the officer in front of her. His uniform seemed a size too big and his face was drawn and ashen but there was no visible sign of any wound. Nor was he consumptive. The dust didn't bother him. Her classmates at the finishing school in Richmond would be revolted simply by the colour of the uniform but she had never quite overcome her first idea that the war was fundamentally stupid. Her father, a Virginian before he came out West, was more intemperate.

She glanced surreptiously at the young colonel

– he was no more than twenty-eight, at most –
and wondered at his future. Or had he used it up
already? If —

'We're slowing down!' That was the thin man,
the surveyor, the one who thought Jefferson Davis
and General Lee should be hanged from the same
tree. The young colonel hadn't reacted to any of
that, not a word, not a glance. But the surveyor
was right about one thing: the coach was slowing.

The stage stop – something to eat, drink and a
chance to walk. Caroline was suddenly aware of
just how cramped her limbs were. She glanced at
the young colonel. His expression was unchanged,
impassive. No, she suddenly realized, not impassive at all. That was show. She sensed an enor-
mous will power at work, keeping up a front.

The coach drew to a halt. She glanced out but
there was only dust to see. Already the fat man
was climbing out of the coach at the other side,
the surveyor following him.

The colonel sprang to life, except it was still
rather jerky life. He opened the door, put the stick
under his arm and climbed down in slow motion,
as if he were thinking it out as he moved. Finally
he was out and offering her his hand. She took it,
allowed herself to be helped down though as a
good horsewoman she really needed no help nor
had she expected much, but there was still

strength in that proffered hand.

Safely on the ground, she looked into his face. It was, if anything, even more rigid than before. Impulsively she reached out and touched his forehead. It was hot, not exactly burning hot, but hot. He had a low fever.

'Are you all right?'

He didn't answer. He was looking round now, the stick firmly planted in the sandy soil, knuckles white from grasping it.

'There's something wrong,' he said.

The dust had cleared and they could see the adobe staging post and part of the corral behind it. There were no horses and no one moving at all.

'I don't like it,' the driver said, joining them. He was carrying a sawn-off shotgun. There was no guard; nothing was carried on the stage but passengers and common mail. The other two passengers were still cut off on the other side of the coach.

'They're normally out straight-away?' the colonel asked. Shaw. That was his name. Jack Shaw.

'Yessir,' the driver replied. He looked worried. ' 'Taint natural, no sir. The Gonzalez family run this stage post. They're always out in a flash. I reckon I'll—'

'Wait. Get the other two here.'

The driver called softly to the other passengers who quickly scuttled around the back of the coach.

'What—?'

'There's something wrong,' Shaw said. 'I'll go with the driver, you two stay here and guard the coach and the young lady. Are you armed?'

The thin man brought out a Navy Colt. The fat man had nothing.

'I have this,' Caroline said, taking the derringer from her handbag. For a moment she thought she saw the mere twitch of a smile on Shaw's face.

'Come on,' he said to the driver, and together they went off towards the adobe way station, the driver matching his pace to Shaw's.

'What do you reckon?' asked the fat man. The surveyor, to whom the question was addressed, said nothing.

'Apaches,' Caroline said, cocking her derringer.

III

It had been bad. They wouldn't let her enter the adobe station until they cleared it out and there had been worse out back. The two other passengers had complained loudly about Shaw not doing any of the digging, saying even an officer and a gentleman should pitch in, but he hadn't risen to the bait. Then the driver had taken them aside, said something to them that had left them looking somewhat abashed.

She'd volunteered to make coffee and caught the driver on his own. It didn't take much questioning to find out that this Shaw was the Colonel Shaw whose regiment had won the Battle of Graylings Landing – she couldn't exactly remember that one: there were so many battles – and won the Medal of Honour. He'd been badly wounded and was on his way to Hacienda Shaw to recuperate.

23

'So he's my new neighbour!'

'Yes, ma'am. He inherited it when his uncle died last year.'

She served the coffee on the long table by the window. Nobody had asked for anything to eat.

'So what do we do now?' asked the driver, looking in Shaw's direction.

He should tell them himself, Shaw thought, but this damned uniform was getting in the way. It was no use to say it's only for convenience, I'm a relict of the army. They wouldn't buy it. Even the two previously rude passengers were now looking at him very respectfully. They'd been told who he was, damn it.

'It's thirty or so miles to Hidalgo?'

'Yes, sir.'

'Open country?'

The driver nodded.

'Could we outrun 'em if we ran into them?'

The driver scratched his poorly shaven chin. 'With six horses, fresh, and a decent start . . . maybe.'

They had four horses, not fresh, and the Apaches – if such they were – were hardly likely to be sporting.

'If we stay put they'll send somebody,' the fat man said.

'Maybe,' the driver said. 'Depends.'

'I don't want to stay here,' Caroline said suddenly.

And then they were all looking at him. Shaw wanted to tell them it wasn't a wise choice. They had something to lose and he didn't . . . but he was too used to responsibility. He said, 'They didn't burn the station and there's food and water left. They could intend to come back this way.'

The surveyor let out a breath, recalling what he'd seen on the corral fence.

'Maybe we could hold them off but I doubt it.' He paused. 'On the other hand they could be waiting for us out there – another four horses to steal – but then I doubt they know the times. Besides, it would have been easier to simply wait for us here.' He paused again. The effort of saying so much had wearied him. Then: 'No, we press on. Feed and water the horses.' He looked to the surveyor. 'Mr Jones, give your pistol to this gentleman. You ride shotgun on top. The driver needs both hands. That way if anybody gets close up they'll face a shotgun and two revolvers.' He reached into his coat and brought out the presentation .32 revolver, gleamingly clean, stubby in contrast with a Colt but deadly enough.

He wondered if Caroline would mention her gun too but she obviously knew what it was really for.

'Any questions?' It had, he realized, turned into a pre-battle briefing. Except he truly hoped there was no battle to come. Outriding the Indians was just talk. They need only shoot one of the lead horses and any chase was over from that moment. With the newfangled cartridge pistols they might have had a chance to hold off half-a-dozen Indians, but it took a long time to reload percussion cap pistols and the fat man was probably a very bad shot . . . . As for himself, he no longer knew.

'Remember to fill the canteens too,' he added.

Someone said 'Yes, sir' but he was no longer listening. He was immensely tired and he needed to sleep very badly. The doctors had all told him he shouldn't risk the journey. They'd been proved right. Except he'd known it even then.

He raised the cup of strong, black coffee to his lips and drank it as if it were strength itself.

IV

'Why are Indians so cruel?' Caroline asked suddenly.

Shaw noticed that the fat man – Wilson, his name was – was looking at him too. He'd helped cut what was left of Gonzalez from the corral fence where the Apaches had built a fire under him.

'Not all Indians are,' he said. 'The Hopi, for instance. And look at us, fighting a war—'

'But we don't torture our prisoners. So why do the Apache?'

'For power,' he said, not minding the talk for once. It helped keep him awake and their minds off what might be out there, though it was an odd way of doing it.

'I plain can't understand it,' Wilson put in.

'That's what they say – for power, a kind of

supernatural power. A kind of spirit stealing.' Shaw paused. 'There's a more rational explanation. It's the way the Apaches live. They're not the most powerful Indian nation, not like the Commanches or the Sioux, which is why they're confined to the semi-desert. And they don't exactly live off the land. They never have. They're bandits. That's what Apache means – it's a Hopi word for enemy. Before we came here they raided the Pueblo Indians and the Mexicans, and for a bandit, terror is a weapon. Just like the Vikings or the Mongols. If your enemy is already terrified, he'll either fight worse or just pay up.' He paused. 'What started out as a tactic has become an article of faith.'

Wilson breathed out loudly, then: 'But even the —'

'Check your window!' Shaw said sharply. He'd been about to mention the children. Caroline hadn't been told there'd been kids there and they'd agreed not to mention it for now.

'Yes, sir.'

He checked his own window. There was nothing to see – thin soil, lightly grassed, a few cacti and the odd stunted bush. What he'd give to see a stand of cottonwoods like the ones at Hacienda Shaw. But at least there was nothing to hide a band of Apaches on horseback. On foot, maybe;

they were good at that; but not even Apaches could disguise a remuda of a dozen horses as a saguaro cactus.

'They should all be wiped out,' Wilson said suddenly. 'Every one of them.'

Even the children? Shaw thought but he didn't say it. He didn't care to debate war of any kind with a civilian. It was too easy to read a newspaper and say, hang him and him. They didn't have to do it. The Apache would be pacified sooner or later – and probably sooner. They were brave despite their faults and they were also the enemy. A soldier shouldn't hate his enemy, just defeat him.

'How much longer?' Caroline asked.

'Two hours,' he said, 'it's open country now.' Any Apaches should be keeping to the rocky hills where they were impossible to trail, but he didn't say it as it would have been too much like tempting fortune.

'We're neighbours,' she said suddenly.

He glanced at her.

'Caroline Lawton – the Lawtons of Hacienda del Rey.'

He remembered fiery old Captain Lawton – captain only by courtesy – owner of the second biggest ranch on the area. That would explain the earlier distance between them. Lawton was about as pro-Confederate as it was possible to be in Union territory and stay out of jail. But Lawton was an old man and he couldn't recall a daughter. Or a wife, though there had been one once.

'My father sent me to school back East. When the war started I moved to Rhode Island, to an aunt's.'

So why was she coming home now? But he didn't ask. He glanced out of the coach window again, saw the same sights as before. The driver was keeping up a vicious pace. Shaw hoped he knew his business. If the horses foundered before they reached Hidalgo. . . .

'Shall I look?' she asked.

Do you know what you'd be looking for? he almost asked, but stopped himself. It didn't matter and it would give her something to do.

'Why not?' he said, and lay back gingerly against the hard coach seat. It would be enormously pleasant to sleep now. It might even give them both confidence, however misplaced, that they were safe. But he dare not risk it. Once he slept he wasn't sure how quickly he could rouse himself. Maybe there'd be no rousing him ever. But he couldn't tell her that.

It would be pleasant nevertheless to take her into his confidence. She was a handsome girl, dark blonde, dark eyes and features too well

30

defined to be called pretty but yet most hand-some. He caught hold of himself. Maybe the weak-ness and languor had subsided these past few hours but that was out of sheer necessity. Nothing had really changed. He still had an ounce of lead lodged near his heart and just waiting to move. He occupied himself checking the .32 calibre pistol his men had presented him in the field hospital. There was even a nameplate:

Jack Shaw

Cavalryman

Liberator of

Graylings Landing

He'd never asked where or who they'd 'liber-ated' the gun from – probably some Reb officer – but it meant more to him than the medal. It was from the men and it was from the regiment – strange how you can get to love an abstract thing like that; even the number 118 was magical to him. . . .

'I can see something!'

He must have been half dozing despite himself for he suddenly realized it was growing dark – bad that: only fools and madmen drive in the dark – but Caroline didn't sound worried, more muffled. The reason was obvious: she was twisted in an unladylike fashion to look forward. He leaned out of the window and saw it too.

It was some miles ahead yet but it was no mirage – Hidalgo was taking its usual counter-measures against the fall of night and the lights burned on the horizon like beacons of hope.

She slipped back into the body of the coach. 'We're safe now, aren't we?'

He hesitated for a moment, then nodded. No Indian wants to fight in the dark a few miles from a town. There probably had never been any danger to them. They'd just touched the edge of horror and driven on.

'Thank you, Colonel,' she said.

'Yes, sir,' Wilson added, 'we owe you our lives.'

Suddenly he hadn't the energy even to argue. That was the problem: once a hero, always a hero. Except the 'always' would be measured in months. . . .

Part Two

Hidalgo

I

It was noon when Shaw awoke. The hotel room looked odd and far larger than it had the night before. A trick of the light. He felt lighter himself, almost well, and he was half wondering if the doctors could have been wrong. Then he started to get out of bed and the pain was back with a vengeance. He sighed: even army surgeons can tell that when a bullet has an entry wound and no exit wound, it's still there. The patient himself was in no doubt.

But he'd no intention of spending his time waiting for it all to end. He'd been truly alive on the coach, horrors and all. No piece of Reb lead was going to deny him that sensation. He looked round for the washstand.

*

34

Hidalgo wasn't a very big or a very old place. Before the Mexican–American War it had been a tiny pueblo but when the Americans moved in it assumed much greater importance. Even its name was new. The original Spanish name had been long and some translator had explained to an incoming American that it was named for a famous hidalgo of Spain. It had been Hidalgo ever since.

Shaw walked its dusty sidewalks reacquainting himself with it, occasionally saying hello to people he knew. No one made a fuss: the Mexicans were indifferent to the war and wandering soldiers were not unusual in a city with its own barracks. They weren't very large, not even large enough to accommodate a full troop of cavalry though the sign outside said otherwise. It also announced that Captain J.P. Rhodes was the commanding officer.

Shaw pointed to it with his stick as the sentry came to attention.

'Is he in?'

'No, sir. Just Sergeant Quinn. That office there, sir.' He pointed in turn.

'I just go in?'

'Yes, sir.'

Shaw smiled to himself. Barracks were usually a highly organized place; not even stray colonels were allowed to wander about at will. But he went to the door and knocked.

'Come in.'

He did so and Quinn, a burly man seated at a desk before a file of papers, came instantly to his feet, saluting. Shaw returned the salute but added, 'I'm a bit of an impostor, I'm afraid. I'm not really a colonel anymore.'

'It was my privilege to exchange the salute, Colonel. Indeed, sir.' he paused. 'Would you care to take a seat, sir.'

Shaw did so, glad to take the weight off his feet. 'I saw the barracks and thought I'd better report what I'd seen yesterday. Is Captain Rhodes—?'

'He left twelve months ago. The last I heard, he's in Andersonville.'

The worst of the Reb prison camps. 'Poor devil.'

'Yes, sir. A fine officer.'

'So who's in charge?'

'I am, sir. We're told to leave the boards as they are for public confidence, sir. Some posts have only a corporal and two men. Here I've seven – mounted infantry but I've made cavalrymen of a sort out of 'em.'

'Like the sentry?'

'Johnson? He's OK when he's off the drink, sir. The reason he didn't escort you in is because I promised to shoot him the next time he wandered off when he's on sentry-go. It's the kids, sir. They wander in and look at the horses. Even go in the stalls. Horses look just the same at the livery stables but. . . .'

Shaw smiled. 'So I'd better tell you, then.'

Quinn took a sheet of paper from the desk and came over to him. 'I spoke to the driver last night and telegraphed a report to HQ. Would you care to see it, sir?'

Shaw took it and glanced over it. It was accurate, more down to Quinn's patient questioning than the driver's observation, he guessed. It also made rather too much of his own part but there was no helping that now.

'Anything to add, sir?'

'Nothing useful. I couldn't tell how many Apache horses there were – the stolen spare horses had covered the tracks and there wasn't time to follow and check, not that I'm very mobile.'

'There were four of 'em, sir, raiding south. They're part of a big raiding party under Long Knife. Colonel Klugg's trying to pin him down in the north but it's hard country to catch Apaches in. But he reckons we'll see no more of them round these parts.'

Shaw noticed that Quinn, for all his respectful-ness, didn't offer to show him the follow up to what he had in his hand. Checking facts was one thing but showing army documents even to distinguished ex-officers was another. A good soldier, Quinn.

'I'm pleased to hear it, Quinn,' he said. 'Especially as I live around these parts now.'

'I know, sir. If I can ever be of service. . . .'

'Thank you.' He got to his feet. 'I'll take up no more of your time. In fact, I think I'll get myself a meal. I can't remember when I last ate.'

'I recommend the hotel dining-room, sir. In fact, there's nowhere else.'

'Then there it is.'

Quinn took him to the gate and saluted him on leaving too.

II

It was hot on the way back to the hotel and Shaw stopped to take off his jacket. Why not? He wasn't a serving officer anymore. The interview with Quinn had driven that fact home. Besides what he could contribute in the way of information was none of his business. And nobody else but soldiers were wearing jackets in Hidalgo. The Mexican half of the population were all sensibly indoors taking their siesta.

Perhaps it was the heat but he didn't feel half bad. He could well manage without the stick and was tempted to toss it aside, but sense won out. With it, he need ask for no man's help.

The hotel loomed up before him, its saloon-style, double swing doors seemingly giving on to a very dark interior. But that was just because the sunlight was so intense. If he stopped and stared at the ground he knew he would be able to see the tiny silica crystals glistening individually. At least he felt cooler in his white shirt except where the jacket hung over his shoulder.

He stepped through the door and halted to let his eyes accustom themselves to the comparative gloom. He heard the voices before he made out the figures.

'We don't want your sort around here, Reb.'

'You never objected to rustling my stock, Carr. What d'ye want now, to steal it all at one go?'

The hotel's ground floor consisted of a restaurant on the right and a bar on the left divided by stairs. The pair of them had met there, Tom Carr on his left and Captain Lawton on his right. They had always hated each other. Carr had a small ranch to the south of town and was reputed to be given to increasing his stock by collecting unbranded yearlings well before round-up. He was an unpleasant piece of work. Shaw recalled that once he had insulted Diego from the Hacienda Shaw and been knocked down in the street for his pains. Nothing had come of it. Only utter fools made a killing enemy of Diego.

'Leave it, Father.'

'Leave it indeed,' Carr mocked. 'You need your women to fight for you, Reb?'

Caroline was standing by the desk which half-nestled under the stairway. Shaw saw the clerk move away, with good reason. Carr was drunk, viciously drunk and he was wearing a gun. So too was Lawton. It was becoming the fashion. And his own was still in his hotel room.

'Father, let's go to our rooms,' Caroline said.

'Father is it?' Carr said, leering at her. 'Well, maybe. Maybe they can't tell the difference in Georgia.'

'I'm a Virginian, sir!' Lawton said. It sounded inane but his face was mottled with rage and he was probably trying to restrain himself for the sake of his daughter.

'There, he admits it!' Carr yelled in triumph. 'A Virginian – a Reb.'

A couple of drunks from the bar side of the hotel were moving towards him now, cronies probably. It could get even uglier and that quickly.

'Captain Lawton is a Virginian – a West Virginian,' Shaw said, softly enough but both heard.

'So what?'

'West Virginia's on our side,' one of the cronies said. 'Has been since '62, split off from Virginia and was made a state.'

It was unwelcome news to Carr who scowled at the crony in question, reducing him to silence. Lawton had the good sense not to deny it though it was a straight lie. Shaw knew he was originally from around Richmond in the eastern part of the state.

Shaw took a pace forward intending to interpose himself between the pair and then lead Lawton and Caroline upstairs.

'Who asked you to interfere, soldier boy?' Carr said, his glance flicking over him and dismissing him completely. Correctly in a way. Carr was a bull of a man. A soldier walking with a stick was of no account to him. He looked back to Lawton, his frustrated anger seeking some new outlet now he couldn't push the old man into a fight as a Reb. 'Yeah, go on and take your Southern whore with you.'

Lawton reacted just as Carr intended, fumbling for his gun. But he had no chance of making it. He had it strapped too high and had no skill. Even drunk, Carr's speed was little impaired. In a second Caroline was going to see her father gunned down in front of her – and it would pass for a fair fight. On oath Shaw would have to say Lawton went for his gun first. The cronies would say that whatever.

He reacted instantly, striking with his stick sword fashion and catching Carr's hand exactly an inch below the wrist. There was an audible crack and the half drawn gun slid from his hand, caught briefly against his holster and then clattered on the stone flagged floor.

Carr looked at Shaw with a feral rage that was more than hate but he made no move. Shaw was holding the stick poised still, like a sword, and even if Carr had never heard of singlestick fighting nor could guess that he was facing a West Point champion, he knew he was staring death in the face. There was nothing he wanted more in the world than to close with this interfering soldier but that unmoving brass ferule and the cold, cold look in his opponent's eyes told him he would get no more than a pace before death took him for its own. He didn't know Shaw would strike for the temple, smashing through bone no less mortally than a bullet, but he knew intuitively the stick was just as dangerous as a sword, and it was in a swordsman's hand.

And then the shock passed and the pain took over. He gave a great whoop of anguish which surprised everyone but Shaw who knew the blow which had looked no more than a tap had broken two bones in the back of his hand. Not cripplingly: they'd mend, but it would be months before he could think of gunplay again.

Carr's cronies led him away, back into the dimmest part of the bar, and Shaw heard his own name mentioned. He smiled inwardly at that:

killing a 'Reb' might well be done with impunity but attacking a crippled war hero with the Medal of Honour was to risk tarring and feathering. Maybe General May really had done him a favour by pressing for the medal for him to make up for his own initial over-caution.

One of the cronies came for the gun. Shaw waved him away. This was the field of battle and the spoils were his to do with as he would. He noticed the pistol had cocked itself on landing. It was in a dangerous condition.

The stick snapped out again – *crack!* Not that of a shot but of the hammer snapping, leaving a harmless, useless implement. He swished it in the direction of the bar and made for the stairs, gesturing the Lawtons before him with a quick snap of the head.

They obeyed unquestioningly and he followed them, veering off at the top to hurry to his own room where he dropped the stick and lowered himself on the bed. He could feel the pain building up. It would be like a cruel fugue, starting low and then building up, repeating itself endlessly. Action and reaction as Newton said.

Carr's pain would be matched at least and he had the advantage of being drunk. But Shaw didn't regret it. Maybe he'd saved no lives on the coach but he had saved a man's life down there and defended a girl's honour. Even if the first was a Reb sympathizer and the abuse of a drunken fool would have done her little harm, it was still worth a little pain. But let it be a little – let it stop!

III

She rapped gently on the door.

'Come in.'

She came in diffidently, leaving the door ajar. It must have been a very good finishing school in Richmond, Shaw thought.

'Excuse me for not getting up.'

'Are you all right?' Her concern was obvious. So was something else. And why not? Hadn't he saved her life and then her father's, defended her honour, and was a wounded hero to boot? Maybe she would have preferred a different colour uniform but women were flexible about such things.

Except it wasn't pity he saw in her eyes. Concern, yes. But something more. He was certain. He felt something very like it himself. It was impossible, nonsensical, but it had happened

46

and it was utterly inappropriate.

He felt the pain stiffening expression from his face. In a few moments he would be without words.

She took a pace forward. 'Let me help. What can I—?'

'Don't you understand?' he said, forcing out the words. 'I came home to die.'

She just stood there, a pole-axed expression on her face.

'I don't want . . . you . . . to see this.'

She hesitated for only a moment and then left, closing the door gently behind her.

Shaw lay there, then remembered the laudanum in his bag but already the effort of getting to it was beyond him. He only succeeded in rolling over. Then he lay there, his chest feeling as if there were a man standing over him and prising his ribs apart with a crowbar.

IV

Long Knife had put Trazz in command of the scouting party but the others looked as much to Manolo as to him. It was a vicious arrangement, Manolo knew, subverting authority, but it pleased him nevertheless. The eight stage horses were only theirs because he had talked Trazz into raiding the way station. Left to his own devices Trazz would have confined their activities simply to looking out for army units or posses, as Long Knife had ordered.

Obedience was all very fine but an Apache didn't make his reputation by simply doing what he was told: he had to do more. And young as he was, Manolo wanted to be more than a simple follower.

He glanced out over the land. Nothing had changed, no movement, no sound of movement and nothing on the horizon. Nonetheless he stayed behind the stunted bushes that provided him with minimal cover. There were limits to independence. Trazz liked him but he would still punish him if he disobeyed him directly and Trazz, stolid as he was, was also quick on his feet and experienced with the knife. Besides, a reputation for casual disobedience was the last thing Manolo needed.

He glanced down at the rifle lying athwart his thighs. Trazz had found himself a better weapon at the way station – his rightful plunder as leader – but he had handed him his own old gun as a pure gift.

It was only a cheap, one-shot Mexican rifle but it was a vast improvement on just the lance he had had before and he ran his fingers lovingly over the well-polished barrel. He had yet to fire it but he had 'dry fired' guns before and knew how to care for them. Every Apache boy learned that. Real skill would take time and anyway he would have a better gun soon enough – which meant he too would have a gun to give away.

That was not only a gift but an opportunity and he would make good use of it. The gift of a weapon, any weapon, but especially a rifle, was a way of forging bonds of obligation. Trazz had been more generous than wise; he had rewarded a competitor, not a follower. He would not make that mistake.

He looked up to survey the desert scene again. Nothing. This was the meeting place but then Long Knife had a day still before he'd promised to be here.

He would be here. He had given his word, given it lightly enough, but for an Apache warrior and leader it was an unbreakable obligation, especially so for Long Knife.

He heard something behind him but did not move, just listened harder. It continued – on the verge of audibility but he knew what it was: a man walking towards him from behind, slowly and carefully. An Apache. No white man could move that quietly.

He was about fifteen feet behind him now, slightly to his left, crouching slightly – it was automatic when you walked in that soft, stalking way. And there would be a steel blade in his hand. He was obviously out to test the younger man and what better way than to illustrate his inattention than by putting cold iron next to his naked throat?

'You can stand up and put the knife away, Trazz,' Manolo said softly. 'There's no one out there to see you.' He didn't turn.

Trazz made a small sound of surprise but said

50

nothing, just came and joined him, not sitting as Manolo was but hunching down.

'How did you know?'

'I just knew,' Manolo said. It wouldn't sound very impressive if he explained. Worse, he would have to admit to guessing, too. Let Trazz put his own interpretation on it.

'I'll relieve you,' Trazz said. 'You can go back to the horses.'

'There's no need now,' Manolo said, pointing to the horizon.

It was hard to see but eventually Trazz made it out. Dust. Long Knife was coming and he was bringing horses with him, a herd of horses. They had all been successful. Trazz stood up and Manolo joined him. They could still see only dust so they both kept by the bush – anyone could have made that dust after all, though neither believed it was anyone but Long Knife.

'He will be pleased with our horses,' Manolo said.

Trazz said nothing, already regretting that he had gone beyond his orders. Manolo could say what he liked but Long Knife would blame him, Trazz, not a youth under his command.

He shrugged mentally. Long Knife had taken horses, so had they: he could say what he liked but he could hardly punish him severely for doing what they had all come here to do. The band wouldn't permit it.

'Look,' said Manolo.

You could see the horses now, and riders – and the sun glinting off the sharpened points of their lances. They would have shrouded them if the army were in the vicinity.

'Come on,' Trazz said, 'let's get our horses and join them.'

Part Three
La Hacienda Shaw

I

The rig had arrived in Hidalgo the night before driven by one of Diego's *vaqueros* – Pedro, a boy of about seventeen Shaw didn't remember seeing before. Apparently he, Shaw, hadn't been expected before morning and Pedro was full of elaborate Spanish apologies, their fulsomeness not in small part due to the fact that Pedro himself could in no way be held accountable for the vagaries of the electric telegraph and its employees.

Shaw liked him. The talk of Apaches in the area simply didn't bother him – didn't he have a *pistola* and a knife? – and he didn't curry favour with the new owner of the Hacienda Shaw. His sun was obviously Diego de Alvarez y Morales, *jefe de vaqueros*. There were other stars in the firmament, no doubt, but only Diego really mattered.

They started off in the early morning, taking it

easy at Shaw's insistence. He'd finally got to the laudanum the day before and the pain was slight now, but the drug had left him with a woozy feeling, like a man on the verge of seasickness.

Conversation was difficult. 'How is Diego?' 'He is well, *señor*.' 'And the Señora?' 'She also, *señor*.' 'And the *hacienda*?' '*Muy bien, señor*.' All with a youthful cheeriness that was almost wearing. Shaw turned instead to studying the land – much the same as the stage had driven across in the wild dash to Hidalgo, scrub on sandy soil, saguaro cacti and here and there grazing cattle. The horses were, he recalled, kept on the grassier northern section.

They nooned only briefly. Pedro wanted to take a siesta but Shaw was wary of lying down and sleeping. His body was used now to the movements of the rig and quite placid. He preferred to keep it that way. Pedro made no great protest. Americanos were strange people but it was well to humour them in their follies. And so, by mid-afternoon, they were on to fair grassland and an hour later approaching the stand of cottonwoods that sheltered the Hacienda Shaw.

Shaw felt tired but content. At least he had come this far: he had come home.

Diego wasn't there to meet him but the Señora

was. She kissed him on both cheeks and led him inside the house. Shaw was shocked to see how she'd changed – the haughty Spanish beauty with raven-black hair and dark, imperious eyes had faded into an old woman in a serape. She led him into the big room and he saw there was a fire in the hearth.

'It's good to be home,' he said, sitting down and suddenly aware that he had slipped into Spanish.

'Your uncle was proud of you,' she said. 'He would have been even prouder if he had lived.'

'I'm sorry I couldn't—'

'No, we understood: duty.'

He suddenly realized, too, that he was in his uncle's chair. He had never sat there, not even as a boy unobserved. It had been sacred in its way.

He looked over the old room – the plastered walls, the polished beams, all very Spanish but uncluttered after his uncle's taste. No pictures, no decorative guns or edged weapons, no framed maps or parchments. The old man had just sat here and thought about the hacienda – the land, the horses, the cattle and the people who lived off them all. Shaw hadn't thought of it before like that, as a responsibility.

'I'll miss him,' he said, and then wished he could bite back the words. How must she feel. . . .

But she only smiled. 'That is good. We should

miss those we have loved.' And he wondered again what their true relationship had been. Officially she was Señora Carmen de Balboa, his uncle's housekeeper, but she had always been simply 'La Señora'. He recalled asking Diego once if she were his uncle's mistress and receiving a cuff from the tough old *vaquero* and the advice that he should mind his own business. Later he'd decided she'd started as mistress and as the passions cooled with age become simply housekeeper. She had been married before, had a daughter, Consuela, whom he recalled disliking for no particular reason, but she was married in Mexico now, the dowry provided – it had been rumoured – by his uncle.

He wondered what to say to her now but she gave him no chance. 'You must rest,' she said. 'I have made everything ready. Diego is taking care of everything outside and I will take care of all inside until you are fit to take up the reins yourself. For now it is enough that you are back in your own home. Your uncle looks down on you from Heaven and smiles.' And suddenly she was in tears and he had to comfort and stifle the question he really wanted to ask – where was Diego?

Yet, as soon as he formed it in his mind, he knew he didn't need to pursue it. It was as if the perspective given him as he was seated here, in this chair, his uncle's chair, provided its own answer. Diego was out on the north range seeing to the horses, keeping them out of the hands of the Apache.

II

'*Hombre de hombre!*' Diego said, grasping his hand. 'It's good to see you.'

He had hardly changed at all. If anything, Diego had got larger. There was some fat there but he knew from experience there was much more muscle. He had seen him wrestle steers to the ground too often to doubt that. And now this paragon called him a man amongst men, a hero.

'Seen anything of Long Knife?'

'Nothing. I think he split his band into raiding parties for horses and when they merge he will take them across the border into the Sierra Madre. But you never know with Apaches so, *patron*, I have brought the herd close to the *hacienda*.'

'Not *patron* to you, Diego. You used to call me *muchachito*, remember?'

'I will again, boy,' Diego said, taking him by the arm, 'but *patron* you are. Accept it. Be the *patron*. Most Americanos do not understand: to be truly *patron* is more than an honour, it's a duty. . . . Your uncle knew that.'

And there was no arguing with that. Diego, perceptive as ever, reverted to *muchachito* and Juanito as they walked round the *hacienda* buildings checking over the milch cows, riding horses and stores. Shaw learnt his family was well – his three sons were still with the horses. He had been a widower for some years but he was now contemplating marriage again with the daughter of a Mexican storekeeper in Hidalgo.

'Caught by a pretty face,' Shaw said.

'No, truth to tell she is old – nearly twenty-five – and plain. But she has a good heart and a good dowry and a man needs a wife. So do you, Juanito.'

'I would make a poor husband at the moment.'

'Ach, good air, good food and better company will mend you soon enough. You are young and strong.' He paused. 'Is very bad, the war? As bad as they say?'

'Worse.'

'At least, for you it is over.'

He could have told him then but something stopped him, not solely the desire not to be watched and pitied but because it would have seemed like casting off responsibility. He had thought of the Hacienda Shaw as a place to come home to; a great property, too; but it was more than that – it was a great duty. And he was never one to shuffle off his duty.

'The Señora? She will not stay long now,' Diego said, as they sat with their whiskies in the great room. 'Here she is – how you say? – a relic. We respect her but she was never truly the *señora*.'
Shaw looked a question.

'*Quien sabe*, Juanito? *Creo que si pero*—' He broke off after that half affirmative, reverted to English. 'In Mexico with her daughter she will have an honest place. Her son-in-law is a *hacien-dado* and she has *dinero* from the *patron*'s will. She will be happier. She has only stayed to see you safe home. As soon as you are well – and bring your own *vera señora* to this house, she will go.'

But I never will, Shaw thought, and was vastly tempted to feel sorry for himself. And yet he had been feeling better these last few days. It could be the laudanum but. . . .

'I heard about town,' Diego said.

Shaw said nothing.

'He is a bad one, that Carr. You should have killed him.'

61

'I got tired of killing,' Shaw said. 'And he wasn't threatening me.'

'Only Lawton . . . who is your enemy.'

'I have no enemies anymore.'

'So long as they know that.' Diego paused. 'I heard the daughter was there. A fine-looking woman by all accounts – a little old, maybe, but an heiress. You should do like me.'

Shaw remembered the look in her eyes. 'As you said – *quien sabe*, who knows?'

That night as he lay in the master bedroom – the Señora had given him no choice: his things had been taken there the first day – he thought about his parents. His father had died in the Mexican War, no medal, no brevet commission, just doing his duty as a first lieutenant. His mother had never gotten over it. She'd tried but even in his memory there was something faded about her. He'd noticed it at the time but it hadn't fully registered. He'd been too young: the world was as it was and sadness was incomprehensible.

Was there that same sadness in him? Maybe it was just the laudanum and the whiskey but he had had less pain these last few days. Besides, if it were only pain, he could live with it. Living was what was important.

He thought about the Gonzalez family at the

way station. Dead, horribly dead, but until an hour or so before they probably had been happy, with hardly a care in the world.

What did that signify?

He couldn't think. Was it the whiskey or laudanum? Probably the whiskey. He laughed to himself. There was a lot of whiskey in the world. . . .

III

He had never quite got back into the swing of steak and eggs for breakfast. It would have been easy to say 'take them away' but La Señora would have scolded him, *patron* or no, so he chavelled them up to make it seem he had eaten something.

He had eaten very little since coming home but his appetite would return. He felt better, a little fevered maybe, but the weight was gone from him. He felt almost strong.

The Señora came into the dining-room with coffee. He could refuse coffee with impunity, he thought, and almost burst out laughing. She smiled back at his smile.

'There is a letter for you, Juanito.'

'From the army for certain,' he said, 'calling me back and making a general out of me.' And then he did laugh.

La Señora looked at him oddly.

'Let's see it then, this famous letter.'

She duly brought it and retreated to the kitchen. He paid no more mind to her, only to the letter.

There was no envelope; it was unfranked, obviously sent by hand and the only address was 'Colonel John Shaw' in a rounded hand, a ladylike hand. A finishing-school hand? Excellent paper too and the wax seal bore the impression of a signet ring but it was too small and he couldn't make it out. He broke it open, screwed up his eyes, and read:

Dear Colonel,

I am writing to thank you on behalf of myself and my father for actions and courtesies of yours known to all three of us. We would tender those thanks personally but hesitate to intrude on your recuperation from wounds nobly incurred in the service of your country. Nonetheless we would not wish you to think us less than deeply grateful and trust we can express this personally at some time in the future. My father also wishes to mention that you will always be welcome at La Hacienda del Rey.

With highest respects,
Miss Caroline Lawton.

Incongruously, his first thought was that it was written with Indian ink on vellum smooth paper, an expensive combination. Well, why not? he thought and let it fall to the table and, as he stared at it, white against the polished mahogany, some acuity returned to his thoughts.

The father had dictated it, he was sure. The invitation was from him, not her. But women were subtle creatures. Whoever had dictated it, *she* had written it. And no gentleman ignored a lady's invitation.

He stood up. He felt surprisingly well. The pain was gone – no, not quite, but it was distant.

'Señora,' he called.

She hurried in.

'Send someone to saddle my horse.'

'But are you well enough?'

He wasn't dressed for riding, he realized, and it would be tedious to have to change. 'A rig, then. Yes, a rig.'

'I will send for Diego.'

'I am *patron* here,' said brutally. 'A rig!'

She took a pace backwards, as if out of surprise. But he didn't notice.

'Yes, *patron*,' she said, 'a rig.'

IV

Tom Carr's hand hurt; even bound up in a sling it hurt like the devil, but it didn't stop him riding, and rather than herd the few dozen scrawny, sickly cattle on his own desert ranch he preferred the more profitable business of rustling – ideally on Shaw range but he was afraid of Diego – 'El Jefe' – and the Lawton spread was big too and much less well policed by its *vaqueros*.

He glanced to his right, saw the scrub and cactus stretching all the way over to box Canyon but not a stray visible. The Lawton herd wasn't a patch on the Shaw herd, he thought. He could do much better, would have if that bastard Shaw hadn't stopped him from killing the old fool.

His hand started throbbing again at the mere memory of it. One of these days . . . but he had El Jefe behind him and he was a war hero and you got hanged for touching his like.

67

'Billy, do you see anything?'

'No, they must all be on the eastern side.'

'Bad guess,' said Johnny Dahl, 'more like over them hills.' He nodded towards Box Canyon and the hills it was set in.

'Yeah,' Carr agreed, examining the ground. It was as bad as on his own ranch. 'We'll noon in the canyon to keep out of sight and swing north afterwards.'

'Sure thing,' Billy Curtis said, starting his horse in that direction. Carr sometimes wondered if Billy was feeble minded and not just slow, but it didn't matter much. Neither of his boys were exactly top hands but they were the best he could get and good enough for herding 'strays' back to the Carr ranch.

They were well on their way to the canyon when they saw the dust on the crest. That meant a rider: cattle raised little dust, they moved too slowly, and never more slowly than approaching noonday.

'After us?' Billy asked, rising in his saddle.

'What for?' Carr snapped. A rustler without cattle was no rustler. All the same, it might be better to stay out of sight. And yet the throbbing in his hand gave him no peace. He was as well riding as nooning. 'If we go up there' – he pointed – 'we'll cut him off. Let me do the talking.' He spurred his horse, knowing the pair would follow him.

It was a rig, driven over-fast on the slopes of the trail, now slowing down. It was 300 yards off but still moving towards them.

'It's that colonel feller,' Billy said, 'the one who bested you.' He didn't quite laugh.

Carr paid him no mind. Billy mightn't be bright but there was nothing wrong with his eyes and if he said it was Shaw, Shaw it would be. He checked his percussion pistol, the belt pulled round to give access to his left hand. He wasn't very good at shooting with his left. Besides, just because there were no witnesses wouldn't make it safe. Diego and everyone else would draw conclusions. His ranch house would burn and himself inside it. And nobody would do a damned thing, not for the killer of a hero.

'Hell, he ain't driving well,' Billy said.

And that was true enough. The horse was doing the driving and that at walking pace now.

Carr spurred his horse towards the rig, drawing up on the safer left side. There was no need. Shaw wasn't armed and barely awake. He held the reins in his hands but very loosely; his eyes seemed to be focused somewhere else.

'He's drunk!' Carr said.

'No,' Johnny Dahl said, having come up on the right side, 'he's sick.' He leaned across and touched Shaw's head. The latter seemed hardly to notice. 'Fever. Pretty bad, I'd say.'

And then Carr had the idea. Despite being hampered by his slung arm he clambered aboard the one-horse rig and took the reins from the unresisting Shaw, pulling the horse to a full stop.

Carr looked around, found the slope he was looking for, then set the rig in motion until they were at the edge of it. It wasn't impossibly steep, quite negotiable by a driver in full command of his senses – though if he were, he'd probably not attempt it – and then, brutally, he pushed Shaw to the ground. He fell relaxed, like a drunk, not hurting himself. That didn't matter in the least.

Carr jumped down and stood over him. Shaw was obviously burning up with fever. It was useful but in a way it was a pity. He reached down and caught Shaw by the neck of his shirt.

'Shaw, can you hear me?' he shouted.

And suddenly there was somebody behind the eyes looking out though the body remained flaccid.

'I'm going to kill you. Me, Tom Carr. I'm going to pay you back, you damned hero – I'm sending you straight to hell!'

'Hey,' Johnny Dahl said, 'they'll hang us all!'

Carr loosened his grip, straightened up. 'For what? I'm not going to shoot him. The guy's sick, not fully recovered from his wounds. How are we to blame if he has a tragic accident?'

'Just hit him on the head,' Billy said, smiling now.

'People don't usually die just from falling out of rigs, Billy,' Carr said. Usually he called him all sorts of a damned fool but for once he was grateful for the chance to explain. 'What if he fell and got dragged now?' He pointed. 'Down there, over those rocks.'

'Smash him to pulp,' Billy said.

'It'd do it,' Johnny agreed.

'So tangle up his feet in the reins.'

'Rope'd be better.'

'But less believable. Besides, there's no rope in the rig.'

'But the reins'll make the horse stop.'

'Not if it's going downslope at a pace,' Carr said, 'and before you ask how I'll manage that' – he reached under the seat and brought out the buggy whip – 'with this!'

Dahl nodded. 'Sure thing, boss,' he said, grabbed the reins and set to work.

It had been harder work than Carr had anticipated getting the horse to go downslope but the buggy whip worked its magic in the end. Once started, the weight of the rig behind pushed the horse forward and Shaw bumped down satisfactorily over the rocky slope until, after about forty yards the horse, hindered by the reins pulling its head to one side, twisted awkwardly in the shafts and toppled the rig over. It lay there, giving out a piteous whinny.

'Reckon it's broke a leg,' Johnny Dahl said.

'I go shoot it?' Billy asked.

'It's just a horse.' He looked to Dahl. 'Do you think he's dead?'

Both of them looked at the crumpled figure, by the overturned rig. 'If he ain't, he soon will be.'

'Maybe I should go check,' Carr said. But the whinny turned into a scream, the peculiar scream only horses can make, and which carries. 'Let's get out of here,' Carr said. He noticed the bloodied whip in his left hand, tossed it downslope and walked back to his horse which was unsettled by the noise. He jerked the reins, pulling its head to one side as he mounted. 'Come on, move it,' he said.

'Back to the ranch?'

'Hell, no. I want to be in town when I hear the news.' He laughed shortly for his hand had started throbbing again. He loosened the reins to let his horse right itself then applied the spurs with a will.

Part Four
The Spent Bullet

I

He was in a dark tunnel and it ended in death. If he had had the energy to be amused, he would have been. It was the oldest of clichés. He would be seeing angels next.

And he did. She was peering down at him, her eyes full of concern and affection but she had no wings. Caroline. If hers was the last face he would see, he was content.

And then there was darkness. Something loud too – the sound of a shot? Then movement. The sky, briefly, and darkness again. More movement. They were interfering with his natural progression towards death and he was annoyed. If they'd only let him be. . . . And then he slept.

He awoke without pain but there was something odd. He tried to move but couldn't. His arms wouldn't obey him – and he was on his stomach. He never slept on his stomach. He tried to tear his arms free and then the pain hit him. His back felt like raw, beaten steak.

He must have made a noise for suddenly she was there in front of him, forcing a smile. 'Don't try to move,' she said.

'Why?'

'Your back's hurt – it happened when you were dragged by the horse.'

He suddenly remembered the noise, the shot. 'You had to shoot the horse?'

'Yes.'

He wanted to make a joke – why not me as well? – but hadn't the energy. 'My spine?' he asked.

She shook her head.

'Then why can't I move?'

'We had to tie your hands so you wouldn't turn over.' She paused. 'Dr Grimes will be back soon.'

He grunted. 'I don't need more doctors. All bloody handed torturers—' And suddenly the darkness was back. The tunnel had become a cave and he was lost in it. He didn't want to be lost. And somehow he slipped into remembering. He saw Carr's face as he looked down at him. He recalled the rocks hitting him, tearing at him. And then it stopped and there was just the screaming of the horse. Diego was right, he thought, I should have killed him. If I live . . . but even if he lived, he'd die. Better to get it done with now, to—

'The fever's gone,' the voice said.

'Is that good?' Caroline.

'Maybe.'

And then something like pain but too distanced to be called pain.

'Extensive lacerations,' the man's voice said, 'some deep – exposed rib under this flap of flesh . . . but I've seen worse. It needs cleaning and sewing up. After that—'

The pain became real. Somebody was dancing on his back. Maybe he was under the horse? No, the horse was dead. They'd been kinder to the horse. Again, darkness.

And dreams. Horrible dreams, confused and violent. Except he couldn't quite recall them. Which meant he was awake. He opened his eyes. The same white bed linen. An odd smell – iodoform. He recalled it too well. He tried, gingerly, to move his arms. They were still tied but more loosely now. He could move all his limbs but it hurt. Though not like before. And his head felt clear. He could even recall the fever – the letter, his mad idea of driving to La Hacienda del Rey, Carr, everything.

'Are you awake?'

He couldn't see him. 'Yes.'

The man came and sat in a chair by the bed. He was about fifty, bearded, going grey, very dark eyes. 'I'm Grimes. I sewed you up last night.'

'I'm obliged.'

'I'll bill you,' Grimes said, half smiling. 'How do you feel?'

Shaw considered. 'Uncomfortable, but I've felt worse.'

'I believe it.' He paused, then: 'I'll show you something.' He disappeared for a moment and then he was back with an enamelled kidney-shaped dish and a pair of forceps. He picked a small object out of the dish, let it fall. It was metal. A bullet.

'Did they shoot me?'

'They—? No, that was an accident, they tell me. This had been in a while. Wedged between your ribs with a mess of rotted clothes too. Your old wound in the front accounts for it. The bullet must have been partially spent. Instead of penetrating the chest cavity it sailed around the ribs and lodged in your back. Hard to tell at the time, I guess. You'd have been one huge bruise. But that would have caused the fever.' He

77

paused. 'Do you want it? A memento?'

A memento mori, Shaw thought. 'No, throw it away!'

'As you will. It'll cause you no more fever. I cleared everything out. The accident did you a favour in a way. It would have been a problem, yes indeed.'

'Then I'll live?'

Grimes laughed. 'I don't give guarantees; anybody can die from anything, but I'd say you'll live. Your back will always look like you've been well flogged but that's all.'

It was too much to take in at once. He said, 'Where's Caroline?'

'Sleeping. I insisted. She helped with the operation. Strong-minded young woman.'

'My hands—'

'I'll leave them as they are. I want you to sleep now. And you won't sleep on your back for a while, believe me.'

'I won't be able to sleep,' Shaw said – or perhaps he just thought it, he wasn't sure. In either case, he was wrong. In moments his eyes closed as if by themselves and he slept – without dreams.

II

Shaw sat leaning on his elbows and looking out from the veranda of Hacienda del Rey at the land before him, more broken with hills than at home. The tea before him stood untouched.

He felt moderately better. His back was still very tender but it was healing well and cleanly and his head was crystal clear. Everyone had visited him here at the Lawtons – Diego, La Señora, the local rancheros he had known before – and he had told none of them about Carr's involvement in his 'accident'. Only Caroline. He wanted no secrets from her. But Carr would wait.

What wouldn't was his life. What next? Now there was a next again. He realized there hadn't been for years. He'd hoped rather than expected to survive the war, but he'd had few illusions. In all truth he'd never expected to see this dry, lovely country again.

And now he was owner of a huge *hacienda* and in a good way to getting another eventually. Lawton already treated him as a future son-in-law and didn't mind the fact that his uniform had once been blue, not grey. As for Caroline, he couldn't have been luckier – except in no way did he believe it was luck.

For all that, he was weary. His change in fortune was simply too great. He often found himself thinking of his old regiment and felt a loyalty to them that was almost overwhelming. But he also owed loyalty to one John Shaw – and Caroline.

As if summoned, she appeared, bringing with her a box of her father's cigars. She looked on slightly disapprovingly as he lit up. He would have liked to stretch back but contented himself with the cigar. She sat nearby.

'You look well.'

'Depends on the comparison. I was all but dead a week ago.'

'So Carr did you a favour.'

'Probably. I don't think I would have ever got here otherwise. I would have died of fever on the trail.'

'Then—'

'Accept that he did me a favour?'

'Not that.' He knew that she would as soon see Carr dead as not: she was frightened for him. 'Wipe the slate clean, perhaps.'

'No,' he said, 'there's a man out there who tried to kill your father, then tried to kill me.'

'Then why don't you denounce him?'

'For what? I was fevered, in a near delirium. So I have a position here, a distinguished military career, a medal, but he's one of their own. They might just give him the benefit of the doubt. And even if they didn't, he'd do no more than a couple of years for assault and then he'd be back harbouring vengeance.'

'So you harbour it instead.'

He shrugged. 'Anyway, if I spoke out, he might not even get to trial. Diego would act. He's not an Americano – they'd hang him. That's why I've got to keep silent.'

'And they wouldn't hang you?'

'I trust not. But forget Carr for now. Let him sweat. There's no hurry at all.' He paused. 'That's not what you're really worried about, is it?' He recalled his cigar, drew on it. A fine leaf.

'You're thinking of going back,' she said, almost accusingly.

'Just thinking, It'll be months before I'm fit for anything.'

81

'Don't.'

He looked at her. The nakedness of the appeal touched him. He said, 'They discharged me for medical reasons. Worst of all, it was their mistake. They'd be loath to admit it. Even if they did, they'd not give me back my regiment, just dump me in an office in charge of forage or something.'

She just looked at him. She knew he'd asked Grimes for a letter declaring him fit. She was certain he was going to use it. He wasn't.

'The truth is,' he said, 'that I'm overwhelmed. I had nothing left and now I've the prospect of all a man could desire. It takes some getting used to.'

'I want you to stay.' Her eyes seemed to burn into him. No feminine wiles, just the same naked appeal. Unless that was a feminine wile itself?

He wasn't sure how to answer her so he didn't. It would be easy to say 'yes' and take everything that was on offer to him. He probably would. But it still all had an unreality to it he couldn't explain. Perhaps he was terrified that it was fairy gold that would disappear in the grasping and he needed time to convince himself it was utterly real. Yes, time.

He smiled at her, reassuringly. He had time, all the time in the world.

Part Five
The General

I

The horses seemed to fill the small, high valley. In its centre an awning had been stretched over poles for shade and under it sat a man in a red shirt, white *peon* trousers shading to grey and tucked into moccasins. He was armed with a Mexican pistol held in a sash around his waist, and a knife – but not the long knife that gave him his name. That remained on his horse, in his quiver, a broken Spanish rapier – but still long enough to be called a sword and remain a stabbing weapon, its point having been stone polished to needle sharpness. But he had no need of it among his own where disputes were settled with words and, occasionally, with quite ordinary knives. It was a weapon solely for war.

Others sat around him, the favoured in the shade, the junior members of the raiding party partly in the sun – no great penance for it was still way off noon.

'Let us go now,' one of the favoured ones said. 'The American General May is gathering his forces.'

'You fear them?' Long Knife asked.

'You know better. They are clumsy and slow but even they can track horses, especially so great a number. They are here' – he took up a stick and marked the ground before him – 'in the north and west, with smaller companies in the American pueblos of the south. If they converge. . . .'

Long Knife looked at the rest, especially the unshaded groundlings. He was their war leader now but nothing else bound them to him – he was neither a hereditary chief nor a medicine man. Only his skill in raiding had brought forty Apaches together. Only his skill in leading would keep them a single band.

'Camisa Verde speaks truth,' he said. 'But what do you say . . . Manolo?'

The young brave singled out was taken aback but not overawed.

'This is my first raid, as you know. I have fought and killed my enemies and taken their horses. I can keep on doing so.'

Together with Trazz he had raided the stage way station in the east, against orders. The horses were good, if on the large side, but it had also been folly. If the Americanos had reinforced the east, it would have ruined his plans.

'No one doubts you, Manolo,' Long Knife said, 'but you are, as you say, inexperienced.' He looked to the first speaker, Camisa Verde, inviting him to speak.

'Our horses demonstrate the courage of all,' Camisa Verde said. 'But horses here are one thing, in Mexico another. I say go now, sweep far to the west and so into Mexico.'

Long Knife paused, as if considering, though the dialogue between himself and Camisa Verde had been worked out hours before. Then, 'There is much sense in that, but does it need forty Apaches to herd two hundred horses? No, and there remain many, many horses in this land. I say this – a quarter of us take the herd, sweep for the west and cross in Mexico and await the rest of us at Aguas Calientes de Bivar while we raid south and east, scooping the herds of the great *haciendas* and driving them before us along the Gran Arroyo.' His foot kicked a route in the dust. 'We move at speed, taking only the best, and yet we should end up with four hundred head at least, altogether a mighty herd indeed.'

They were silent a moment and then they began their acclamation of the plan – and Long

Knife. He basked in the praise a while then ended it with brief instructions, naming the the party to take the horses west. It included Manolo and his companions. They would miss the great raid – he need not say that, nor did – but he did say they were being given a sacred trust. Punishment and praise combined. The others noted it and he rose in their estimation.

He was gaining great honour. Soon he would be *the* Apache leader – men from all the sub-tribes would come willingly to fight alongside him. Then would be the time to meet the Americanos and rout them. But now was not the time to talk of such things.

'We will all meet in Mexico and drink tiswan together. Go now.'

He watched the boy Manolo wander off towards his horse. He did not walk with the slow pace of anger but with the easy pace of a man who accepted his lesson. He stood up, turned to Camisa Verde.

'We ride.'

II

Shaw had gone out to test the Army Colts he'd had fitted in leather sheaths on the front of his saddle. On due reflection the presentation .32 had seemed a little on the light side. If he met up with the likes of Carr again he intended to be well prepared.

In the event he hadn't fired them. Nobody could hit anything from a moving horse and there had seemed little point in disturbing his mount to prove it. In the week that had gone by since his fall and his return to La Hacienda Shaw he'd done little but potter about the house. He was much fitter but still not fit enough to ride with the *vaqueros* without being a drag on them, and while he was now assuredly in command of the ranch, he'd found no occasion to change anything at all.

La Señora was blaming herself for letting

herself be overridden by him in his fevered state and had put off her journey to Mexico, so she was still running the house with her unrivalled precision. And Diego required no lessons in horse and cattle rearing from his former pupil.

Shaw knew well enough that the art of leading was, when nothing needed to be done, to do nothing. So had his uncle. But he was finding it at once too hard and too easy. Grimes still refused him that letter which might, just might, get him back into the army, and which he might, only might, use if he got it. Caroline visited regularly and he was glad to see her. In a way everything was settled between them, and nothing was settled.

He was, he thought, trying to reach a new understanding with the world. To be without pain ought to make him deliriously happy but he'd already half forgotten how it had been. The war, too, was almost forgotten. The newspapers arrived. He sat down to read them and somehow never got beyond the first paragraph.

It was as if he were in a kind of limbo. The landscape was certainly right for it, he thought, glancing over the lightly, grassed land to the immediate south of the house – the worst grazing of all. Even the saguaro cacti were stunted.

His horse raised its head as if it had suddenly realized where it was. Over the next rise and the house would be in sight. He stopped to light a cigar. He patted the horse's neck. 'I'd give you one too,' he said, 'but you'd only eat it.'

But after a few moments he urged the horse on without indulging. He could smoke it at home, in the great room, maybe with a glass of cognac. Probably without, though.

And then he topped the rise and saw the soldiers – seven of them, all standing by their horses with glasses in their hands. Hospitality of a sort had been provided. An eighth horse was tied up but unaccompanied. The horse of the officer in charge, presumably, who would be waiting for him in the great room.

A matter of urgency, he wondered? But he didn't set his spurs to his horse's flanks. It didn't feel urgent to him.

III

Brigadier-General May was a large, heavy man but when Shaw entered the great room he was on his feet in a flash, saluting. Out of uniform, Shaw could only bow slightly in return.

That bloody medal! he thought. It was the custom for Medal of Honour winners to receive the first salute from all ranks. But May had over-done it a little. He was out of uniform after all. Which meant he wanted something. But why else would he be here?

'Welcome to La Hacienda Shaw, sir.'

'Thank you.' He looked Shaw over. 'You look OK,' he said.

'Yes, sir.'

'Bloody surgeons got it wrong again. But for a change the victim lived. I've heard the tale of Dr Grimes taking the ball out of your back.'

Shaw nodded. 'I didn't know you were in this part of the country, sir.'

'Commanding it. I relieved Klugg ten days ago. He should be in the Shenandoah Valley now, commanding a division.'

Shaw said nothing. May was still wearing the single star. The promotion hadn't been his.

'Sit down – and forgive my presumption in telling you what to do in your own house and you not a serving soldier.' He flipped back into his chair, grinning. 'You're right in what you're thinking. I've been put out to pasture. I know you thought I was too cautious at Graylings Landing and now Grant thinks I was somewhere else, too. I disagree in both cases.'

Shaw sat opposite him. 'Can I offer—?'

May pointed to a glass on the table beside him. 'I helped myself.' He paused, then: 'Tell me, Shaw, what is a regiment of cavalry?'

Shaw just looked at him.

'Stumped you, eh? I'll tell you then – it's a loaded gun. One shot too. You don't learn that till you're a general; until then you're one of the working parts. Fire it too early and you've missed: too late and it's no use.' He paused. 'I was right at Graylings Landing and so were you. The opportunity came, you took it. I was right later, too, but that's another matter and of no matter now because this backwa-

92

ter I've been sent to is also at war – with Long Knife.'

'I know, sir.'

'Heard about that. My predecessor kept good files.' He reached into his pocket, brought out a map and tossed it to Shaw. 'Have a look at that.'

Shaw did so. In the top centre there was a question mark and below it, sweeping south-east and south-west, two great arrows, roughly drawn.

'I don't know exactly where he is and I don't know which way he'll come. I've over thirty forts and barracks to man and three-quarter strength regiments to do it with . . . and mounted infantry at that. You might have noticed I haven't an aide. He's now commanding a company in the west because I'm shorter of officers than I am of enlisted men. Now do you see why I've come here?'

'I'd make a poor aide, sir.'

'I doubt that but no matter. I can manage without one. What I need is a brigade commander.'

The military department they were in was due a division of three brigades, a minimum of six regiments. In a European army it would be due a major general to command it but the Republic had always been wary of high rank. Even Grant had only three stars.

Shaw said, 'I was hoping to get my old regiment back.'

93

'No chance of that, boy. 'They'd not know you now anyway – too full of replacements. Besides, while the Union hasn't given me many men, it has given me many powers. I can restore you to your old rank by fiat. Or keep you from it forever.'

'Shall I order dinner, General?' Shaw said suddenly.

'I don't know I have the time—'

'Make it, sir. I'll feed your men and horses too. ' He called for La Señora, then turned back to May. 'Cold roast or sizzling steaks?'

'Yes, why not,' May said, then adding a little sadly, 'but the cold beef it will have to be.'

Shaw stared at the map. It didn't make for cheerfulness. If Long Knife took the easterly route, that would be through here and Caroline's and a dozen other ranches, a potential thousand plus head of horses. The big *haciendas* could afford to restock but the ranches couldn't – and that was assuming a lightning raid with no casualties. It could be otherwise. Shaw could still recall what they'd buried at the way station all too clearly. . . .

But Long Knife could move west, which would make the Fifth Territorial Auxiliary Regiment (Volunteer) as useful as tits on a bull. Not that it amounted to much yet. The fact that May had come to him having last seen him dying told him all he needed to know concerning how desperate he was. Add that at present the total forces of the regiment were the cadre of eight soldiers in Hidalgo plus himself and the desperation was confirmed. May hoped he could take *vaqueros* from the ranches to build up to at least company size – no more than a hundred Apaches were expected – and had empowered him to impress them if needed. But he wouldn't. He wasn't about to ride against Apaches with pressed men behind him.

He picked up the orders from the table where May had left them and riffled through them. May had delegated a great deal. He had powers to do just about anything, short of seceding from the Onion. Which was safe enough given the means to hand. He folded the papers and the map together and started for the master bedroom. If he were to be a colonel again he'd better put on his uniform.

IV

Quinn was waiting. He'd even changed the name of the C.O. on the notice board.

'Did you get any recruits, sir?' was his first question.

'Not yet. The *vaqueros* are doing more good where they are for the moment. I want volunteers from town. How many can you horse?'

'I've two spare horses, sir.'

'How about rifles?'

'Twenty Springfields and more than enough ammunition, sir. No uniforms and all the rations we buy locally.'

'Long Knife can probably do better on the quartermaster side than we can,' Shaw said. He shrugged. 'No matter. Most of 'em have guns and horses anyway. Will they join up, I wonder?'

'What's the bounty, sir?'

'Free food and ammunition in the field but no cash. I've pretty wide authority. I can just about hang 'em but I can't tax 'em.' He paused. 'Hell, I can afford to offer one myself – twenty-five dollars on enlistment.'

'On discharge, if I might suggest it, sir, That way we'll get 'em sober.'

'Good thinking. So where do we start?'

'You've not done this before, Colonel?'

'No.'

'The saloons, sir.'

Shaw laughed, then: 'Quinn, take off those stripes.'

'Sir?'

'I need a second-in-command and that's a captain's appointment, at least. It's only a temporary brevet rank so there's no pay, but it won't harm your record any.'

'Thank you, sir. I can find a spare pair of bars. If you'll excuse me a moment, sir. . . .'

And five minutes later he was back, wearing a captain's jacket and an officer's kepi. 'Captain Rhodes didn't have space for everything. I don't think he'll mind.'

'No matter if he does, Captain,' Shaw said. 'Come on, I'll buy you a drink to celebrate.'

They got nineteen volunteers – most of them

better at drinking and gambling than anything, but they could all ride and shoot which was a start. He'd raised the bounty to fifty dollars when the earlier figure hadn't aroused much interest so he'd cost Hacienda Shaw the better part of a thousand dollars, unreclaimable, but it would be money well spent if it saved the Shaw remuda.

And despite what Quinn had said about uniforms they'd managed to outfit them all to at least look like cavalry – the general store had dark-blue work shirts and navy serge trousers and he'd signed a chit for them. They were even happy to unload their stock. He'd also issued Springfields to those who wanted them and for those who preferred their own guns the general store had provided sixty rounds apiece, also signed for by him. A Medal of Honour winner had little trouble getting credit, even for the army.

Kitted out, and with six livery stable horses rented for those that hadn't their own, he assembled them to the south of town. Three of the regular troopers had been promoted temporary sergeants and the 'regiment' now had four troops – Quinn's, with the remaining troopers, who had some idea what it was about, and three others who hadn't a clue.

They exercised them for about half an hour without major accident though with much shouting, and then Shaw took Quinn aside.

'What do you reckon, Captain?'

'Colonel, I can lick 'em into shape – just give me a month then we'll take Richmond.'

Shaw laughed. 'I can give you two days so go easy on 'em. I know they're sworn in under military discipline but if they ride off we haven't the men to chase them. Impress on them to do what A troop does unless their sergeants tell them otherwise – and pray.'

'I reckon these bars don't come cheap,' Quinn said reflectively. 'Where'll you be, sir?'

Quinn was quick, Shaw noted. That was to the good. A regiment was only as good as its officers.

'I'm going to round up some more volunteers – buckaroos, *vaqueros* and real horsemen.'

'We need 'em, sir. How many men do you want to take with you, sir?'

If the general could manage without an side, he could manage without an escort.

'None, just keep an eye on the telegraph and if anything comes in of importance send a rider out to the Shaw Hacienda – if I'm not there, they'll know where to find me.'

'And if Long Knife turns up while you're away, sir?'

'Use your own judgement.' He softened it. 'I don't reckon he will. And you might be able to use this.' He delved into his pocket and brought forth a roll of Union scrip, peeled off around a hundred dollars.

'Buy 'em some whiskey tonight. And tomorrow night too.'

'Dutch courage,' Quinn said.

'We can use any kind we can get,' Shaw said.

'No,' Diego said, 'I do not wish to join the Yankee army.'

'There's no chance of anyone being drafted to fight in the East,' Shaw said.

Diego looked around the great room. 'Thirty years ago, when the de las Casas owned this *hacienda* and I was a boy learning to be a *vaquero*, the *señorito* – the son of the house – was made a captain in the Mexican Army and he took the *vaqueros* off to war. Against the Americanos. They never came back. I swore the same oath and was given the same uniform but they left me here because I was too young.

'And then we became part of los Estados Unidos and your uncle came; he treated me well – better than the de las Casas. Never would I have drunk whiskey in the great room with them as I did with him and I do with you now. I never saw this room then, nor any inside the house. I was a *peon*. I kissed their hands and took what scraps they gave me. Today I am a man – *el jefe de vaqueros*. I have respect but. . . .'

Shaw offered Diego a cigar, took one himself and lit it.

'But?'

'Your uncle told me everything. You have not.' Diego looked straight at him, the cigar unlit in his hand, the dark eyes fixed on him.

'True,' Shaw said. 'But I have not lied, Diego, not intentionally at least. As you say, I simply haven't told you everything.'

'Then do so now,' Diego said, lighting his cigar.

'Ay, pobre muchachito! Si habia sabido. . . .' His voice hardened. 'And as for Carr—'

'Do nothing,' Shaw ordered. 'I will take care of Carr.'

Diego smiled and Shaw realized just how coldly he had said the name. It was odd to hate the man who had, albeit unintentionally, saved his life but he did.

'It is personal, I understand. But if I catch him rustling on the *hacienda*. . . .'

'Shoot him by all means.' No one sheds a tear

over a rustler caught *in flagrante delicto*. 'Just don't hang him.'

Diego nodded. '*Comprendo.*'

He would agree to join up now, Shaw knew, but why should he? The chief of vaqueros was a nice title but it meant no more at heart than foreman. Why should he risk his life for wages in a land that had become half foreign to him?

And suddenly, seated here in his uncle's chair in this room, at the very heart of the *hacienda*, he knew what should be done. Almost as if he could think his uncle's thoughts . . . and yet, if his uncle had wanted it done, why hadn't he done it himself? The answer was obvious – he had intended Shaw to do it himself.

'Tell me, Diego, what do you think of Valle de Naco?'

'It's fair range, good for horses, but it is difficult to get to – we have not exploited it fully.'

'There is land enough for a ranch?'

'*Sí, es un vero ranchito* – it could provide work for four, five men—' He broke off, looked to Shaw.

'*Es tuyo,*' Shaw said, 'it's yours. My hand on it.' And he extended his hand. 'Whether you join up or not.'

Diego put down his cigar and whiskey and sat very still. Then, after a long moment, he reached out and took Shaw's hand, rising out of his chair

103

as he did so and pulling Shaw to him, kissing him on both cheeks.

'*Mi Juanito – mi hijo!*' And Shaw almost wept at that: the man he loved as a father loved him as a son.

When Diego had left he was not only a *ranchero* but a captain of volunteers commanding the second battalion of the regiment – E, F and G troops combined, collected from volunteers from La Hacienda Shaw and the *ranchos* and *ranchitos* to the south and east of it – Diego estimated fifty men, all well found, with their own horses and guns. Not parade-ground cavalry but little worse.

The 'regiment' was approaching the establishment of a regular troop. Now Shaw had only to ride north to Hacienda del Rey and recruit H troop. But he had one thing to do first.

He went into the kitchen and found La Señora with the cook, a maid and Jeronimo, the old *vaquero* who did odd jobs round the *hacienda*. He led them all into the great room and took paper and pen and wrote out a quitclaim for Diego, his heirs and assigns, for El Valle de Naco, for the sum of one dollar and many services, already paid. He had them all witness it. It was La Señora's turn to kiss him then.

He gave the paper to her to keep for Diego. The

old *vaquero* himself had been content with a handshake but a man who was going to war needed more than that for the sake of his honour.

He sat again in the *haciendado's* chair and finished off his cigar and knew he had served more than his own honour. He had made the *hacienda* stronger too. El Valle de Naco brought in little profit being too far out. And Diego's sons would have sons and they would be welcome to Hacienda Shaw as *vaqueros*, and friends. He had gained many friends. . . .

But he still had an enemy – Long Knife, a brigand even among Indians but a skilful one. A man who might yet kill him and destroy everything he loved and had found again. But not without an almighty struggle.

He stood up. He needed to be away.

VI

'Do you go into battle wearing that?' Caroline asked.

She was looking at the medal. 'No, just recruiting. I'd forgotten it was there. But why not?'

She was silent, but he knew what her silence was saying – because you might die.

Well, he wasn't afraid of death. Or even so much dying anymore, though he'd prefer it without pain. But he couldn't say that to her.

'I didn't bring the war here, my dear,' he said. It was the first endearment he'd tendered her. It hadn't seemed necessary before. Feelings were strong, the knowing sufficed. But it melted her.

'I'm sorry,' she began, rubbing at her eyes.

'Don't worry, I'm hard to kill. If the whole South couldn't manage it, I doubt a painted savage will do more.' He couldn't tell her that in battle luck played the major part for the individual. But at least Long Knife would have no batteries of nine pounders. He reached out and took her hand. It wasn't fairy gold after all, just warm and soft and genuine. He raised it to his lips.

'If the departing warrior may . . .' he said, and kissed it.

'Oh, don't be silly!' she said, and would have returned the compliment rather more heartily but her father returned, oblivious apparently to the by-play.

'They're readying themselves now. They all volunteered, but I've kept eight, leaving you twenty-four under Pablo Guzman, my foreman. Good man. Incidentally, I'm paying them all the bounty myself. No reason your outfit should stand all the expense.'

'I'm obliged, sir.'

'I'd come with you myself, even wear blue to do it,' Captain Lawton said, 'but I'm too damned old to be any use.' He paused only briefly. 'But if that damned ragamuffin comes here, don't worry about Caroline. I can defend my own house – and will! You needn't worry about your girl.'

Caroline flushed scarlet at that. Shaw couldn't quite work out why but he was both pleased and blissfully untroubled by the fact of it.

'I never doubted it, sir,' he said. He had, but he didn't now.

'I'll leave you to make your farewells,' Captain Lawton said and tactfully departed.

VII

Caroline watched them ride off, Jack Shaw in his uniform, the rest in their workaday clothes, but this was no workaday thing. They were going to war.

She'd seen soldiers going to war before back East, but it had been different. The war had been a long way away and this was on her own doorstep. And she'd had nobody riding with them she cared about.

'Come on, girl,' Captain Lawton said when they were almost lost from sight, hidden by their own dust. 'Jack's a tough 'un. He'll be back.'

How did he know? But she let herself be led back inside.

'I'm having a drink,' Captain Lawton said. 'Do you want one?'

He'd never asked that before. In fact, he'd

hardly asked anything. She'd been away so long they had been almost strangers for a while after her return and then, very suddenly, she'd been truly home again. And they had been close – she'd even told him about Jack. It was her father who had told her to write – as if he'd known.

She wondered briefly if he really could have known it would turn out all right, as it had . . . but it was obvious he couldn't have done. And yet maybe age brought a wisdom with it she couldn't yet understand.

'Are you sure?'

Lawton sat down, a glass of bourbon in his hand. 'That I'm going to have a drink or Jack'll be all right?' He was smiling. Then, seeing her expression, he became a tad more solemn. 'I'm surer of the first than the second, but the chances are very good.'

'You've fought the Apaches yourself,' she said, remembering. That was how he got the unofficial title of 'captain' – he'd led the ranchers against them.

He nodded. 'Nothing this big but I know how they fight. You don't have battles with them so much as chase them – and usually they're too fleet for you.' He paused, sipped his drink. 'Come to think of it, if they fought any other way they'd be wiped out. They're very few and we're not.

110

That's why I'm not worried. Altogether your Jack will have a company of a hundred men which, while it might be pretty small beer in Virginia now, is a damn' huge army out here. This Long Knife will take one look from a distance and high-tail it for the Mex border. That's my guess, at least.'

He was humouring her, she realized, but was he humouring her with the truth?

'I hope you're right,' she said.

'So do I.' He glanced at her. 'Maybe I did wrong sending you back East for so long.'

'I would have been a tougher frontier woman if I'd stayed?'

'You're a Lawton and quite tough enough. I saw you watch over your young man day and night.' He paused. 'No, I was thinking of myself. What I missed. But it seemed the sensible thing to do after your mother died. . . .'

'I'm home now,' she said. She didn't add – and I mean to stay but her tone did it for her.

'Good girl!' Captain Lawton got to his feet and then walked over to her, kissed her on the cheek and pressed the glass into her hands. 'Here, finish this for me. I've work to do and so have you.'

And no feminine collywobbles had better get in the way? The thought made her angry and yet it was a challenge too. She raised the glass to her

111

lips and drank. She had never tasted bourbon before and the strength of it surprised her unpleasantly, but she didn't allow herself to show it.

Lawton just nodded, then walked over to the gun cabinet. He opened it – it was never locked – and took out one of the gunbelts, which he strapped on, and then took up a long gun. He paused then, suddenly looking very serious, and finally took one of the loose six-guns from the bottom of the cabinet and came and put it on the table beside her.

'You know how to use that?' he said.

'Of course I do.'

'Well, I said I'd defend Hacienda del Rey and I intend to. If the Apaches come, use it, and save the last bullet for—' He broke off.

Caroline was shocked for a moment. She'd been thinking exclusively about Jack and forgotten that aspect of things.

'It won't come to it, I'm sure,' Lawton said, 'but—' He broke off again.

Caroline picked up the gun. It was loaded. An unloaded gun was useless on the frontier. And it was heavy . . . but not too heavy.

'Remember to cock it before you—'

'I haven't been away *that* long!' she said indignantly, but she didn't cock it. Walking around holding a cocked gun was folly.

'Hell,' Lawton said, smiling broadly, 'I reckon you haven't really been away at all. Let's go and find our *vaqueros*, those we have left. We've a *hacienda* to protect.'

VIII

From the window of his office, Sean Quinn watched the despatch rider leave then went back to his desk. The papers were mounting up, he noticed. A regiment generated infinitely more paperwork than a company, even if it was only provisional and at cadre strength. The accounts were in a mess, too.

But he had no time for them now, nor much inclination either. He hadn't slept in three days though he didn't feel all that tired. The bars on his shoulders saw to that.

Quinn was a career soldier, which was why he had been left out here on the frontier. When you stripped the companies of their officers you needed good NCOs to leave behind. He'd thought he'd spend the war behind a desk and was half ashamed that it didn't worry him more. In the army you went where you were posted and stayed there until you were posted elsewhere, but when he'd volunteered and been turned down, he'd been secretly relieved. No medals for him, but no even chance of being killed either.

So why wasn't he afraid now? The answer was simple – the captain's bars Shaw had so casually awarded him. Every farm boy joining the army hoped to be made an officer one day though few indeed ever were. Quinn didn't fool himself that General May would confirm the rank. This was for one battle only . . . unless he did very well indeed. Then he might let it ride as a wartime rank and afterwards – the end of the war was in sight – he might just get kept on as a second lieutenant and slowly work his way up to captain again.

It was just barely possible. It depended on what kind of officer Shaw was, a glory hunter or a good cavalryman. But mostly he needed to be lucky. And if some of that luck rubbed off. . . .

Whatever, he was grateful to him. However it all turned out he would see action as a captain in the United States Army, the very thing he'd dreamed of as a recruit.

'Damn the accounts,' he said aloud and, retrieving his kepi from the stand, strode out of the office headed for the field of glory.

Part Six
The Campaign

I

Raiding, Apaches travelled ideally with a remuda of up to four horses apiece, which meant they could be swift both in the attack and in retreat. But as their intention was to steal horses, including broken stock, Long Knife had decreed only sufficient spare horses were taken to ensure that no one was left afoot. As they were moving through the hilly, eastern part of the region to avoid detection – the great *haciendas* only sent their men into the hills for round-up – that too slowed their pace. And they were hungry: the parched corn was running low.

But Long Knife was well satisfied. They had met with only one Americano – not really an Americano at that, a *peon* in their employ – and the knife had ensured his silence. His burro had been added to the communal remuda and tonight, Long Knife had decided, it would feast their bellies.

He had been waiting for a secluded valley

where a fire could be risked but he had found something better, with grazing enough for the horses too. No tiswan, but that was to the good: the Apache knew only one way to drink – to excess. Fine enough *after* the battle, not before.

But he did not expect much in the way of battles. The great houses he would leave alone. They could furnish much plunder but with the soldiers behind him – and before him, for all he knew – it would only be a hindrance. Horses were the ideal plunder, valuable and swift moving.

'Here,' he said, and dismounted. He need say no more. The band would do everything needful, the younger men preparing the fire and butchering the burro, the elders sharpening their lances, checking their bows and the fletchings of their arrows, a few polishing their guns.

There were only two principles of raiding – speed and deception, and the latter was only a substitute for the former, though sometimes a very needful one. Tomorrow they would come down on to the plain and begin scooping up the horses of the Americanos, fighting where they had to, running with their living plunder otherwise.

The burro made a noise somewhere between a snort and a scream as its throat was cut. Long Knife smiled. There would be meat in all their bellies tonight – but not too much.

119

II

The despatch rider caught up with them five miles out of town – he was one of the recruits, little more than a boy but a fine rider and very proud of himself, a Springfield in his saddle sheath and percussion revolver stuck in the dark-blue sash around his stomach.

'I was sent to Hacienda Shaw to catch up with you, Colonel. Captain Quinn sends this.'

'This' turned out to be a telegram from May.

LONG KNIFE ATTACKED RANCHO DURDE TUES. 11.40 BELIEVED MOVING SOUTH.

The Durde ranch was thirty miles north so he could be here anytime. Long Knife was moving fairly fast and May was writing very carefully. He had given no orders, just information. At a later board of enquiry he could disavow anything Shaw did as failing to carry out the *verbal* orders given earlier. Likewise any success could easily be attributed upwards.

Shaw didn't care. He wasn't in this for May, the Union or right or justice: he was fighting for his own hearth and home and those of his neighbours. He took out a stub of pencil, licked it, and wrote on the back:

Diego
Meet me at Box Canyon 5.00 p.m. Bring what forces you have ready. Apaches on the move.
Jack

He handed it over and said, 'Take that to Jefe Diego – it's Captain Diego now, and stay with him.'

'Yes, sir.' And the boy looked on as troop H – aside from Shaw not a single one of them with a single military item to his name – set off again in the direction of Hidalgo, watching with absolute intensity as if he needed to remember every last detail of his first campaign. Finally he applied his own spurs.

'He'll founder that horse,' Guzman said, glancing back.

'No,' Shaw said, 'he'll get through – he's too

young to believe in failure.' And regretted it instantly. That was a word that should not be spoken or even thought now.

Guzman, the del Hey foreman and now first lieutenant of volunteers, just laughed. Then: 'I was looking over your shoulder, Colonel – why Box Canyon?'

'It's the only major feature between the two *haciendas*,' Shaw said.

'We could take the men there now, save wear and tear on the horses and send for Quinn to join us.'

It was a sensible suggestion but Shaw shook his head. Never split your forces unnecessarily in the presence of the enemy. Maybe Long Knife was still twenty miles off but he wasn't going to risk it. Besides, he wanted the regiment to ride together if only for an hour or so. The Apaches had ridden together for the whole of their lives.

III

'There are three men and a hundred head of cattle,' Camisa Verde said. 'They are a hundred paces in from the mouth of the canyon. They did not see us.'

The canyon was poor grazing for that many head. Why take cattle there?

'*Vaqueros*?'

'Americanos,' Camisa Verde replied.

'Maybe they are stealing cattle,' Long Knife said, and would have laughed at his own joke if it were fitting for an Apache to laugh when out on a raid.

'What do we do?' Camisa Verle asked.

Long Knife considered. He had sent five braves to raid the Hacienda del Rey with instructions to bring their plunder back to this box canyon. It was convenient to have somewhere to hide before the attack on the second *hacienda*, too convenient for three Americanos to make any difference.

'Take them – by stealth. And keep the cattle penned in.' That last was important. If they stampeded the dust would look too like a band of Apaches and could draw the Americans to them.

Camisa Verde nodded. 'I shall go myself. One of them at least will be alive to talk.'

Long Knife waited patiently, listening to the talk of the waiting band. The Hacienda Durde attack had been a failure – the *vaqueros* had corralled their horses and fought hard for them. And with the army only hours behind he hadn't dared draw it out. But nobody had been hurt and the band was still in good spirits – a sizeable remuda from the del Rey and the like from the de las Casas *hacienda* – a man called Shaw owned it now, odd unpronounceable name – and they could ride to Aguas Calientes de Bivar with 400 head quite easily. That would suffice. He would be the greatest Apache leader alive.

Then he saw Camisa Verde walking back from the canyon mouth. He gave no order, just started his horse forward knowing the others would follow.

All three were alive but one was moaning from a knife wound to the stomach. Long Knife gestured. He was stilled. He looked to the other two, a big man with his arm in a sling and a little man with

124

a glazed look to his eyes – not fear but stupidity, he judged.

'Why are you here?' he asked in Spanish – no white man spoke Apache.

The big man scarcely spoke Spanish either but he had a few words.

'Cattle – looking to cattle.'

Long Knife looked at him and was not impressed. A man should not show such fear in the face of his enemy. But he had another reason for disliking him. A mere glance at the ground confirmed that the stock had not been brought here for forage. This man was a thief. When the Apaches raided, thieves often thrived, hiding their depredations under the cloak of war. This man had been stealing more than cattle, he had been stealing their honour.

Camisa Verde asked, 'The knife?'

They had time to make the death hard. Fire was best for that but impossible. They couldn't risk the smoke. But the cattle gave him an idea. He spoke to Camisa Verde and the rest.

'Take cattle. We go,' the big man pleaded, not understanding.

Long Knife didn't bother to answer. Already the braves were herding the cattle back and the two men with them.

IV

'You can't leave the town unprotected!' the mayor protested.

He was a fat man, a saloon keeper, very probably a pimp too. Shaw didn't give a damn what he thought but it was still a fair point. He'd skimmed off the town's fighting men. If he beat Long Knife but some Apaches made it this far south and raided here it would spoil his men's victory.

'Very well,' he said, 'I'll leave a troop here.'

'Thank you, sir. I knew I could—'

Shaw turned on his heel, looking for Quinn. He found him on the other side of the street talking to Guzman. 'Captain, I've promised the mayor a troop—'

'But Colonel—'

'I know. Promote another of your regulars to sergeant, give him three men and tell them to

126

make a show of themselves on the north side of town. If the Apaches get this far south and see them, they'll assume there are more and avoid the place.'

'Shall I tell them that, sir?'

'Why not? Otherwise they'll find a bar to lean on. In fact, stress that they're safer if they're seen, not otherwise. Maybe they'll believe it.'

'I'll make sure they do, sir.'

'I'll give you ten minutes, then we're moving out.' He turned to Guzman. 'Make sure your men's horses are watered – but not too much.'

Guzman just nodded.

An unnecessary instruction, Shaw thought: Guzman and his men needed no instructions on how to treat their horses. They were good *vaqueros*.

'What about a drink, Colonel?' Quinn asked. 'Can I let them have a quick one in the saloons?'

'Once inside they'd be the devil to get out,' Shaw said. 'No, but get a bottle and pass it around. Charge it to Hacienda Shaw.'

A little more Dutch courage would do no harm – so long as the emphasis was on little.

Despite Quinn's attempts to keep the various troops distinct, the little army clumped together like a rather disreputable posse. The townsmen were of the most dubious mettle though they made up the numbers, but its real strength was in Quinn's corporal's guard of regulars and Guzman's *vaqueros*.

These were the detachment's weaknesses, very evident to Shaw's professional eye, but it had a strength too – its firepower. Nearly everyone had a revolver of some sort and at close range that amounted to over 200 shots in a few seconds – if they held together.

Quinn joined him. 'I can't keep 'em in formation, sir.'

'Don't try. We're cavalry by courtesy of being astride horses, no more. A huddle might even be for the best. We lead and they'll follow.'

Quinn nodded. 'There is that, sir.' He paused. 'I see you've got no sabre, sir.'

Shaw pointed to the twin Colts. 'These will be more use.'

'You're still welcome to mine, sir.'

He shook his head. 'No, it will do me more good in your hands, Captain. And I have that.' He gestured towards the walking cane still in the otherwise empty rifle sheath. 'My marshal's baton.'

Quinn laughed. 'It'll sound well in the report, sir.'

Unless this little regiment ran like hell at the

first sight of the enemy with its heroic colonel trailing after them, he thought. But that couldn't be said even jokingly. Instead he took out his watch and, after a quick calculation, raised his hand.

'Dismount! We've time before our rendezvous at the box canyon. We'll walk our horses.'

The townsmen were only too glad to walk for a while; the regular soldiers were expecting it; only the *vaqueros* were surprised. And as Shaw led his little troop across the bright, hot and somewhat dreary plain, his riding boots biting his feet and the sweat turning his blue serge uniform into a damp rag, he realized that for all he was leading a weak and uncertain force against a cruel and formidable enemy, he was utterly content. He was home at last.

It was hard to judge how many they were but the predominant blue gave away their nature – the Americano Army. A troop, maybe. More men than he had. And they were walking their horses. *Vaqueros* never did. But worst of all they were driving up his line of retreat and had come upon him hidden in a box canyon – a canyon with no other exit.

Fortunately they had not seen him yet and the screaming of the prisoners had stopped a while ago. They could not know where his band was. But if they did. . . . He pushed the thought aside. If they did he was beaten . . . and he was not beaten.

'The cattle!' he said. 'Bring the cattle to the mouth of the canyon but keep them just inside.'

Camisa Verde looked at him blankly for a moment, then he understood. 'But the braves at

Hacienda del Rey? The horses?'

'They will hear the shooting and detour,' he said. Perhaps. They could take care of themselves. Or not.

Even as they talked the troop to the south mounted up again. Camisa Verde needed no further spur. He disappeared back into the canyon.

Long Knife lay there in the dust a moment longer. The horses were lost. If they were lucky they might collect some on the way to Aguas Calientes de Bivar but no great number. Yet horses were, after all, merely horses. If he could defeat the US Army on the battlefield that was worth more than a thousand, ten thousand horses. With something almost akin to joy he moved back to the rocks that marked the entrance to the canyon.

VI

In the moments when they first saw the cattle Shaw understood what May had said about generalship. He had in effect two loaded pistols, one to hand – the troop – and one due in an hour – Diego's men. Did he fire one now or hold off? He knew what choice May would have made, the cautious choice, the losing choice. He chose instead to risk disaster for the sake of victory.

The men had only seen cattle. You expect to see cattle on a *hacienda*. It took them a few moments to register that they were being stampeded towards them and that behind them were Apaches with lances, bows, guns, knives and a hunger to use them.

Shaw ripped the cane from the sheath and, wielding it like a sword, cried, 'Follow me!' and charged.

If he had given them a second longer they might have balked but Quinn followed and Guzman so the rest put spur to flank. It wasn't a conventional cavalry charge – walk, canter and then charge only at the last but pell mell and hell for leather at the start.

Some might have peeled off even then if they hadn't seen that the yelling madman, stick still raised in his hand, wasn't heading directly for the oncoming herd but across it, for the gap between it and the canyon.

It was a close run thing. The lances of the Apache had been liberally used and the cattle were moving quickly. Those long horns, each set backed by a third of a ton of sheer terror and wild fury, would have ripped through any body of horsemen in the world. But a herd of cattle could not be turned on a dime. The Apache had brought them on the run and so left a 200-yard gap. With the herd between them and the oncoming soldiers they couldn't even fire at them.

When Shaw stayed his panting horse at the canyon's mouth he had not lost a single man.

'To the back!' he yelled, gesturing with the cane. It would have been folly to try and make a stand at its entrance. The cattle could be turned and used as a battering ram too.

He stayed there till the last of the troopers had

133

passed, then followed into the relative gloom of the canyon, right on back to where the ground rose in a ridge, yielding to a bowl surrounded on three sides by sheer slopes.

Quinn hadn't waited for orders but was already dismounting his men and forming a defence line on the reverse slope of the ridge, detailing other men to picket the horses.

'Riflemen first,' Shaw shouted. 'Save your pistols until you need them.' It took a while to load a percussion pistol.

Quinn joined him. 'I hope you know what you're doing, sir.'

'So do I,' Shaw said and laughed. Several of the soldiers looked up briefly. One of those delegated came and took Shaw's horse. After a moment Shaw realized that left him armed only with the cane which was still in his hand. It didn't matter. He turned to Quinn.

'I reckon we've ten minutes' grace. Then they'll try a *coup de main* – come in heavy and try and take us. We beat that off. After that, if they've any sense, they'll scuttle. If we're lucky, they won't and before the hour's out we'll have them between two fires—'

'Sir!' It was one of the new-made sergeants, his face white as a sheet. 'Come and see, sir. For God's sake, it's—'

'Quiet down, soldier,' Quinn said abruptly. He looked to Shaw who said:

'Why not?'

They had buried them in the sandy soil with only their heads out and then crowded the cattle over them, probably prodding the steers with their lances to get them roiling over the pair. One was already dead, his throat cut by a hoof, blood like a shroud around him covering even the filth. The other was alive, kicked partly out of the ground. The Apaches hadn't dug deep. He'd been tied with rawhide in a foetal position, almost into a tiny ball which must have been agonizing in itself but it was the face that had sickened the trooper.

There was no face – no eyes, nose, hair, ears, and you could only tell there was a mouth from the broken teeth that occasionally showed through the slowly bubbling blood.

Shaw saw something else. The right arm had been in a sling, now in shreds, and the right hand was bandaged – Carr. What had he been doing here with the cattle? The question answered itself but didn't matter anymore. There were sounds coming from the poor, damned creature.

'What's he saying?' Quinn asked.

'What would you be saying?' Shaw snapped, turned and saw everyone was standing, forgetful of their peril, looking on. All to the good.

'This is what awaits the losers,' he said. 'Don't lose.' He turned back, looked to the soldier who had come to him.

'Finish him.'

The soldier hesitated. The creature gurgled. If he had had a gun Shaw would have shot him there and then – out of pure pity, all thoughts of vengeance lost.

Crack! The skull fragmented into something that might never have been human. Quinn put away his revolver. For a moment Shaw thought he was going to say something but he didn't. Nothing needed to be said.

On reflection Shaw went and found his horse and took both pistols, shoving them into his belt.

Part Seven
Long Knife

It was half an hour before the Apaches came. Shaw guessed they'd been trying to round up some of the herd to repeat the trick but was unworried by the prospect. That gun had already been fired and it was single shot. The cattle would be too dispersed and too weary – and the Apaches weren't good *vaqueros*. If they wanted to exploit the situation they'd have to do it all by themselves.

The sensible option when someone had so obviously put themselves into the perfect trap was to wonder why and then leave, but most commanders, he knew, would only believe the enemy stupid. He hoped Long Knife would do just that.

Long Knife had never believed the Americanos to

be stupid but he was a leader by the fact of leading. His instincts told him to leave but the band was humiliated at being tricked and he knew if he pressed them to leave even the loyal Camisa Verde would rebel and attack with the larger half of the band. Camisa Verde would lose – he had courage and skill as a warrior but he was no leader. Yet if he allowed it Camisa Verde would be the brave Apache who died and he would be Long Knife, the warrior who ran away.

He tried to think of other ways – sending men to the heights to fire down, but that would take an hour and there was little cover at the top. Simply waiting them out was impossible. There were troops to the north of them for certain and maybe others converging on them too. The choice boiled down to going in on horseback or on foot. The twist in the canyon made the latter hard. They need merely train their guns and wait. It would have to be an overwhelming charge.

They were already muttering. He had been too successful before. They had all been blooded. They had the 'power' of their dead enemies and they were anxious for more of it. There was nothing else for it.

'Now,' he said.

II

First there was a rumbling sound, the clatter of unshod hooves on the stony ground augmented by echoes, and then the Apaches had turned the corner and were charging four abreast, their lance heads glittering in the shadow of the rock walls.

Shaw had no need to give the word of command. The rifles crackled instantly and then the pistols started crashing out. Forgetting his own strictures he drew himself, emptied one Colt and would have emptied the other if the Apaches hadn't backed off, leaving eight of their number dead, and six horses. A few more pistol shots cracked out as some fired into the fallen Indians, other stilling the wounded horses.

'Cease fire and reload!' he yelled, his voice preternaturally loud now the reverberations of battle had died away.

140

Suddenly the ramrods were out and the guns were reloaded. He drew the other pistol. Now was the time for Long Knife to attack again and, as if the thought had conjured it up, they were back, screaming and firing their guns, unfired on the first charge, but to no effect that he could see. A man firing from horseback was making noise, nothing more. And the corpses of their own men and horses formed a barrier. One Apache jumped over it and Shaw aimed and fired directly at him.

The Apache's face turned red then the horse and rider were behind him. Others were leaping down from their horses and rushing at them with lances and knives. Shaw fired again, not even attempting to direct the battle. He fired until the second Colt was empty and then flung it at the mêlée in front of him. Somehow his hand found the stick and he slashed out with it, without science or skill, just the blind fury of battle.

And then it was over. The Indians still horsed, he guessed about sixteen, retreated again. He looked around. Everyone left alive was reloading with fervour. An attack now would be fatal, he knew. These were not infantrymen with bayonets. If the Apache broke through their line it would be the end but fortunately the thought didn't conjure up the reality.

Why? he asked himself but answer was before

him. Half the band lay dead before their guns. Two of their own were dead and three men were wounded but nobody was caring for them. Rightly so: their lives and the lives of them all depended on recharging the firepower that had stopped the fury of the Apache attack in its tracks.

He should reload himself but he hadn't the energy. His back ached as if he'd just been flogged and he felt weakness in every limb. He hadn't been fit for this battle, he thought, and would have laughed aloud if his mouth and throat weren't too dry to do more than cackle, and the stench and fog of spent powder had turned the air into a ghastly miasma.

Nobody moved. The guns were all reloaded, waiting. And nobody came. How long had they waited? It was impossible to say. Battle does strange things to the sense of time. It seemed hours but it was more likely only minutes.

Someone was groaning – in the pile of the Apache dead and dying or from their own ranks? He set the matter aside. Only the next attack mattered.

And suddenly he was sure it wasn't coming. They'd beaten them back. His mind was functioning like a commander's again – the Apaches had been fewer than he'd expected, thirtyish he estimated, and they'd taken more than half of them out for only limited casualties. They weren't coming back.

'Captain Quinn!' Shaw shouted, turning to look for him but Quinn made no answer nor ever would. He lay a dozen feet from him with an Apache lance through his heart.

'Guzman – leave two men with the wounded. Get the rest mounted. It's our turn now.' They were words of victory but they only strained his parched throat.

He went for his horse, not running because he couldn't but parodying the motions of a man running. Others were doing likewise. He mounted up first, assuming the lead automatically, skirting the Apache dead at a walk, his horse snorting with communicated fury or maybe just gasping from the stench of burnt powder.

It could have been a ruse, a trap, but instinct said otherwise and it was right. The canyon was empty save for two more Apaches, lying dead and abandoned, their horses taken by their *compadres*, and at its mouth, the body of a white man who looked very white indeed, his throat gaping and the blood like an overblown shadow before him.

He rode to the entrance and saw instantly there were no ambushes waiting for them – the

Apache were already 300 yards away, a much diminished raiding party ... and beyond them, half a mile away, another party approached.

Diego.

His men joined him, spreading out till they were stirrup to stirrup. They were a real regiment now, blooded together. But the Apaches held his attention. What would they do? Diego looked to have fifty men, *vaqueros*, *rancheros*, minor *haciendados* – in their way as good irregular cavalry as the Apaches, not so fleeting but better armed and more heavily horsed, more effective in the shock of clashing charges.

Split, he thought, break up, try to break out on the flanks – just for a moment putting himself in the place of the Apaches. Cruel they might be but they were fine soldiers. Those two charges against a wall of fire had been magnificent in their way.

Diego was moving forward slowly. Sensibly. If the Apaches broke, it would be easier to mop them up, and if they charged they could still be met at speed for the niceties of a cavalry charge build up – walk, canter, charge – weren't in his mind. They'd just go hell for leather. But no – it was the Apaches who were slowing.

And then they halted. Shaw waited for the twin burst for the flanks but it never came. Instead they turned about and started moving back. To the canyon. Towards them.

It was a suicidal tactic. Even if they made it there was no relieving force for them. They'd die in the canyon. But even to get there they had to pass through his men.

He considered ordering them to dismount, to repeat the previous tactic but there was no cover and if even one or two of the enemy got through, the wounded and those caring for them would be at their mercy. And yet meeting them at the standstill was impossible too.

On impulse he took out his watch. It was ten minutes to five. Had so little time passed? Whatever, Diego was on time. They were 150 yards off now. He slipped his watch away, glanced to either side, seeing faces he didn't recognize, and said, 'On my word we'll engage the enemy. Use your pistols.' He waited. Eighty yards. Sixty yards. Then he used the word he hadn't risked before.

'Charge!'

His horse responded to the mere touch of the spur, leaping ahead. The Apaches were almost upon him and he didn't know if he were alone or not and couldn't even look back to find out. He was suddenly aware that his pistols were still in the canyon, thoughtlessly left unloaded, and all he had was the silly stick under his arm. For want of anything better, he took it in his right hand then the first Apache was upon him, jabbing with a lance. He brushed it aside and then he was past and the next Apache just disregarded him and then there were no more. There was a crackle of shots behind him and he turned to see the twin charges had turned into a confused mêlée which the Apaches were getting the worst of – this was the one occasion when you could fire mounted to some effect, though he guessed several of his men would suffer from 'friendly fire'. And then one of the Apaches singled him out, a medium-sized man in a red shirt and long moccasins wielding what looked like a short sword.

With astonishing speed the Apache was on him, slashing out with the blade. Automatically he turned the blow with the cane and saw the Apache wheel about with the same unbelievable speed and come at him again, the sword levelled high.

Shaw spurred his horse, met him, knocked the sword to the left and lunged forward over the head of his horse, braced hard against the stirrups, the ferrule of the stick serving for point, and caught the Apache full in the neck.

Shaw felt it tear into the gristle of the larynx, saw the Indian catapult over his horse's hindquarters almost wrenching the stick from his

hand and then he was past, leaving Shaw to real-
ize that this must have been Long Knife himself.
Well named, he thought coldly, because he had
used the sword like a knife – a long knife. Cavalry
used sabres and not rapiers for good reason.

Then he wheeled about and saw it was all over.
No Apache remained horsed and half a dozen of
his own men were down, dead or wounded he
could not know. The victors were reining back
their horses, pistols still in hand though he
doubted even one of them held a single charge.
Again, sheer firepower had won the day.

He glanced back. Diego's men were almost upon
them, making some kind of noise. Cheering. He
looked at the stick in his hand, saw it on the wall,
a plaque below: 'With this cane. . . .'

He dropped the reins, took the cane with both
hands and, with a convulsive effort, broke it and
threw the two fragments far away.

III

Diego was talking to him but the words seemed to be coming from too far away for him to make them out. He saw the *vaqueros* caring for their own fallen – and putting extra shots into each of the fallen Apaches. He ought to stop it he thought, but he was too tired to speak and it was probably kindest anyway. If any had survived they would only have hanged them. All the same. . . .

'. . . Hacienda del Rey—'

The words impinged on Shaw's consciousness. The tiredness fell away. He looked to Diego. 'What's happened there?'

'An attack. They sent a rider.'

'Caroline's all right?'

Diego reached across to him, held his arm. '*No sé, mi hijo.* But she should be. They were only after the horses.'

148

For a moment the ache in his back, the dryness of his mouth, the total utter weariness of battle and its aftermath together with this news seemed to be about to overwhelm him. But he fought back. 'After the horses . . .' Diego had said. Horses, horses, horses. . . . He tried to think of what he must do and then he realized.

'Diego, I need a fast horse, the fastest.' He was already dismounting. Diego called to one of his *vaqueros*.

'You also need a gun,' Diego said, taking one of the pair in the sash around his waist. A red sash. Diego had taken his captaincy seriously. But why not? It was serious, as was his own command. These men were still his regiment, his responsibility. He looked around, saw Guzman, called to him.

'Sir?'

'Take the men back to town. There's another band of Indians to the north. I'll take Diego and half his battalion' – how easily the formal words slipped out, he thought – 'and see to them. The rest will go with you.'

'And the dead, sir?'

For a moment he thought he meant all the dead, but Guzman would leave the Apache dead for the coyotes without a doubt. But he'd see to that later, have them buried in the canyon. Like dead cattle. No – they'd have their memorial. The canyon would finally acquire a name – Apache Canyon.

'Let's ride,' he said.

As they crossed the trail he found himself recalling the rig and the slope – and Carr. It was as if the hatred and the horror had cancelled out – to nothing. Except Carr's ranch would soon be up for sale – cheap. He might buy it. Yet he knew he didn't care a cent for land at the moment but he couldn't let himself think what might have happened to Caroline. Everything would have been for nothing if—

He stopped himself, gave a touch of spur to the flanks of the fine animal he now rode and which was serving him valiantly. Diego was still half a length behind but the others were stringing out badly. If the Apaches ran into them like this . . . his military brain began to upbraid him but the devil with that. The Fifth Volunteers was still a legal entity and he was still a legal colonel but that was all, mere legality. It would never fight again. He was now only Jack Shaw of La Hacienda Shaw with Diego and his *vaqueros*, riding to the aid of his neighbour and—

He saw her in the distance. She was standing on the veranda of the *hacienda*. He rubbed his powder-smoke grimed eyes. Yes, it was her, apparently unharmed. So was the *hacienda*. And no sign of battle.

'Slow down,' Diego commanded from beside him, having made up the half length, and Shaw did, cutting back to a canter.

'*Gracias a Dios*!' Diego said, seeing her and Shaw could have echoed that but his throat was too dry. Only then did he remember his canteen and reached for it, spilling water over himself as he drank.

'*Cuidado* – have a care,' Diego said.

But the water wouldn't choke him. Nothing could hurt him now, he thought, and flinched away from it – only a fool dares fate.

'Caroline, are you—?'

'I'm fine,' she said, as he dismounted and went to her. 'There were only half a dozen of them and they were only after horses. Father and the remaining *vaqueros* fought them off. They only got away with three horses.'

'Anyone hurt?' That was Diego.

'My father. A bullet grazed his arm but he's fine.' She half smiled. 'He's very proud of himself.' She looked to Shaw who was standing a yard from her, looking at her. 'My God Jack—'

He knew what he looked like, blackened by

powder, skin grey with weariness and eyes vacant. He had seen men come out of battle before. And he had not been fit for it in the first place. He went and sat down in the veranda chair he used before.

'I'm just tired,' he said.

'He killed Long Knife, wiped out the band,' Diego said, still on his horse.

Shaw felt oddly annoyed at hearing that. He knew Caroline would think no more and no less of him whether he had succeeded or not. And he had no wish to tell her the details himself, not now.

'Do you need us here, *señorita*?'

She smiled at Diego, shook her head.

'I'll leave you, Juanito. We've horse-thieves to deal with.' He smiled wolfishly.

Shaw nodded. The rest of them had caught up now.

'You'll need fresh horses,' Caroline said. 'I'll ask Mr Guzman—' She broke off, remembering, and suddenly unsure if she were talking of the dead or the living.

'He's OK,' Shaw said. 'On the way to town.'

'Then just help yourselves,' Caroline said.

Shaw watched them go the corrals, Diego with them, then glanced back at Caroline. She was waiting, he knew. Knowing she was safe was enough for him at this moment but she wanted more. He was expected to lift himself from his comfortable chair and take her in his arms. That he was filthy and probably smelt worse than his horse was no matter. How would he tell her that he couldn't; that if he did he would probably break down and weep?

The devil with it, he thought, getting slowly to his feet – he'd risk it!

IV

Aguas Calientes de Bivar was an unwelcoming place, a low, poorly grassed valley set in the foothills of the Sierra Madres. The warm springs of the Spanish name were truly named but of no great size and the water, while not quite poisonous, was malodorous and bitter to drink. At one time a rich *haciendado* had built a lodge around the pool but it was roofless now, long abandoned like the valley itself.

No *peon* could make a living off the poor soil and it wasn't even worth the trouble to bring cattle here. They lost more weight on the trail back than they gained cropping the lower reaches of the sparsely grassed valley.

But there was just enough grass for their horses for a few days and, best of all, it was equidistant from the two Mexican *haciendas* south of the border, a little lost valley all on its own. It was safe for a few days at least, on the long way back into the Sierra Madres.

Trazz was on watch, seated on the highest point of the ruined lodge, the rifle he had taken from the stagecoach station across his knees. But he wasn't thinking of the dead Gonzalez family. All his attention was focused on the entrance to the small, northern pass that gave access to this valley.

Pedrito, the youngest of them, was hidden in the high rocks there with a view over the plains to the north for half a day's ride. If he saw anything he could report back in minutes, but Manolo had insisted he signal first – and so someone had to watch.

Trazz thought it excessively cautious but that was a good trait in an Apache so he bore his stint of watching with unblinking patience, not expecting to see anything. It took time to drive a great herd of horses anywhere. You could run them off quickly enough but you needed to let them forage after that otherwise they turned to skin and bone.

A knife flashed in the sun, four times. Apaches – no enemies visible. Unhurriedly. Trazz stood up and then began to climb down to join the rest. He could see Manolo looking at him but he didn't call out.

Patience too was a warrior virtue.

They were all waiting for the newcomers when they came to the lodge – just three of them, without even spare horses for themselves. None of the three was injured – they wouldn't have made it if they had been – but they were bone weary. They had been pursued to the border by soldiers and *vaqueros*. After attacking the Hacienda del Rey and being driven off they had doubled back at night to the box canyon and seen the bodies. Mago, who had been leading, had seen Long Knife's among them. Thereafter he had led his little band south; the soldiers had spotted them the next day. It had been touch and go after that but he was obviously proud that he had led his depleted little band to the meeting place, here at Aguas Calientes de Bivar. He presumed to lead here too.

'Long Knife would want us to—'

'He is dead,' Manolo said abruptly. 'His name will be spoken by us no more.'

They all looked to him. It was a true saying. A dead Apache's wicki-up was burned, his possessions destroyed, his name no longer spoken, so as not to disturb his spirit. And by saying this Manolo was assuming the leadership of the band. If they would accept him.

'There are still two hundred horses here,' he went on. '*We* lost none on the way here. Now there are fewer of us . . . but so much greater honour for those who return.'

No one spoke. That was all true, but Manolo was

young, perhaps not ripe for command yet. Normally Mago would have been their choice but he had come back to them almost as a fugitive – and the bearer of bad news. A leader should be luckier.

It was Trazz who decided. 'Manolo speaks well,' he said. 'I will follow him.'

The acclamation followed, not enthusiastic but unanimous. Even Mago accepted it, or seemed to, for he looked to Manolo and asked, 'What do we do now?'

Manolo was not short of an answer. 'Tonight we feast and drink tiswan. Tomorrow or the next day, we move south. The worst of the horses we sell to the Mexicans for guns and food.' He paused. If he had been Long Knife's kin he might have pledged vengeance now but it would have been personal only, not binding upon anyone else here. He still could as a way of assuming Long Knife's mantle but he judged it both unnecessary and pointless. Long Knife was dead, he was alive. That was enough.

Instead he said, 'One day we will go back. The Americanos have many fine horses.' Then, briskly: 'Mago, kill your horse. We will eat it.'

Mago, still hunkered down in weariness, glanced up at him. It was his chance. He could challenge the new leader, take control if he won. But Manolo was fast and fresh too; he was tired and slow and he just did not care that much for leadership anyway.

'Yes, Manolo,' he said, drawing his knife.

Epilogue

It was four days since the battle and two since May had stopped by on his way to Hidalgo, disappointed that he would not go with him so he might bask in reflected glory. Shaw didn't doubt that after it had all been written up quite a lot of it would have stuck to May anyway. Maybe that was unfair. He owed his medal to him and that did give him one advantage – an automatic presidential nomination for his son to West Point. But it might be wise to get married first. He smiled to himself and poured himself another cup of coffee from the porcelain jug on the table. It was a good place, this veranda. In fact, he rather liked Hacienda del Rey. He and Captain Lawton were quite pals these days since the latter had got himself the slightest of nicks from a stray bullet and fancied himself a fellow warrior.

158

His cigar had gone out. He tapped off the ash and looked for the lucifers, stopped when he saw the horseman. He was a mile off and riding slowly but he was wearing Union blue.

Another summons to Hidalgo? The last one had been verbal and May had been amply answered by Caroline who thought him far too weak. He wasn't but she made a very useful, indeed unanswerable advocate.

She must have seen the rider too for she joined him. He didn't rise. She'd forbidden it in almost the same tone she'd employed with General May.

'I wonder—' she began.

'You never wonder in the army,' he said, 'you wait.'

She scowled a little. He still was in the army and she didn't care for the reminder.

'I've a despatch for you, Colonel,' the rider said, having dismounted and marched up on to the veranda. He was a corporal from May's detachment. Shaw took the proffered paper and read it, then looked up at the soldier.

'Yes, sir!' the corporal said, grinning.

'Do you want a drink, Corporal?'

'Thank you, sir, but I've got to get back.'

Shaw nodded. 'I'm obliged – and thank General May on my behalf.'

'Yes, sir.' And then he marched off the veranda,

mounted up in a soldierly fashion and rode off.

'Well?' Caroline asked.

'It's army business. A copy of a telegram.'

'Oh,' she said tightly.

Shaw relented, smiling. 'It reads: "This day General Lee surrendered the Army of Virginia at Appomattox to General Grant".'

She didn't take it in for a moment, then: 'It's over.'

'All bar the shouting. I'm effectively just an unemployed ex-soldier. I'll never make it to general.' He paused. 'Our son might, though. If, of course, we had one and he were legitimate.'

And suddenly she was weeping. He wasn't sure if the cause were the war's end, or the defeat of the South, his proposal, or his ham-fisted way of phrasing it, but he already knew what to do about it.

He got to his feet. . . .